BRIANNA, MY BROTHER, AND THE BLOG

Brianna, My Brother, and the Blog

JACK WEYLAND

DESERET
BOOK

SALT LAKE CITY, UTAH

Library of Congress Cataloging-in-Publication Data

Weyland, Jack, 1940–
    Brianna, my brother, and the blog / Jack Weyland.
       p. cm.
    Summary: Upon returning from his mission, Austin meets Brianna, the girlfriend of his brother Robbie, now a missionary himself, and as their friendship blossoms, he begins to learn what makes a relationship work and posts his findings on a blog.
    ISBN 978-1-60641-140-7 (paperbound)
    [1. Mormons—Fiction.   2. Interpersonal relations—Fiction.   3. Blogs—Fiction.]   I. Title.
    PZ7.W538Bqq 2009
    [Fic]—dc22

                                                                                    2009009631

Printed in the United States of America
Worzalla Publishing Co., Stevens Point, WI

10   9   8   7   6   5   4   3   2   1

To Sherry

Thank you for making it so worthwhile for me to make you laugh.
I love to sit nearby when you're reading something I've written.
For me, when you laugh, it's like I've won the lottery
(which, because I don't gamble, will never happen).

Acknowledgments

Many years ago, as a freshman at Montana State University, I was enrolled in a required English class taught by Verne Dusenberry. After a few days, he approached me after class and said, "I'm starting a new section of this class. We'll only meet once a week, and everyone will get an automatic A. Would you be interested?"

I loved the idea of getting out of work, so I enthusiastically said yes.

True to his word, we met once a week. We talked, we read, we discussed, and we wrote. There were no tests, and all of us received an A.

It was not until years later that I finally realized what a gift Verne Dusenberry had given me. He gave me confidence that I could write and that my ideas were as good as anyone else's.

Much of all that has occurred to me in terms of my writing has come from his early influence in my life. Sadly, he passed away before I even thought to thank him.

Acknowledgments

This is a little late, but thank you, Mr. Dusenberry. I am extremely grateful to you.

I also express my appreciation to Shari Pack for teaching me about harps as I wrote this novel.

Chapter One

Wednesday, June 11

"And this is Brianna!" my mom said proudly.

I had no idea who Brianna was or why my folks had brought her to the SLC International Airport to welcome me home from my mission.

I figured she might possibly be one of my cousins from Nebraska. The ones we never see. Except for one thing. In our family, we're all born ugly. Only after a few years do we get better looking. This girl looked as though she'd been born beautiful and then improved after that, so obviously she couldn't be a cousin.

She was only a couple of inches shorter than me. Her good posture made me wonder if she might be a dancer. All this, with long, straight, reddish-brown hair, thick-forest-like eyebrows and lashes, and either brown or green eyes, I couldn't tell which.

Some girls have thin lips, but she did not. They were,

1

well, not thin. Actually, since I was technically a mission-ary for at least a few more hours, I was embarrassed to have even noticed her lips.

However, what surprised me most was that she seemed so excited to see me. "Welcome home, Elder!" she shouted out. I was just going to shake her hand, but she practically threw herself at me, wrapped her arms around my neck, and gave me a big hug. I panicked and looked over to my mom for protection.

"It's okay, it's just Brianna," my mom said. Everyone seemed to know what that meant. Everyone except me.

"Hopefully, she'll be a part of our family once Robbie gets home," my dad explained proudly.

"So little Robbie has a girlfriend?" I asked.

"I wrote you all about it, Austin," my mom said with her familiar, slightly accusatory tone of voice.

On my mission, my mom's letters came every week. Unfortunately, it took about that long to read them. Each one was eight to ten pages long. Reading them was made more difficult because my mom has terrible handwriting. So, the truth is, I hadn't always read every page.

I decided to fake it. "Oh, of course, it's Brianna, Robbie's special friend!" When I shook her hand, I was surprised she had such a strong grip.

"Brianna will be with us the rest of the day, but then she'll come back on Saturday and stay overnight with us," my mom said, "so she'll hear your talk in church."

"We already think of her as part of our family," my dad said with a big, goofy grin on his face.

"What year in school are you, Brianna?" I asked.

"I'm a sophomore."

"Good for you. What high school do you go to?"

She gave me a strange look. "Actually, I'm a sophomore at BYU."

"Really? Well, you seem so young to be in college."

"I'm twenty."

"So you're the same age as little Robbie then, right?"

"'Little Robbie' is now six-foot-five," she said with a grin.

"I wrote you about his growth spurt," my mom explained.

I wasn't going to make that mistake again. "Right. I remember," I lied.

We lived in Layton, Utah, so it didn't take very long to drive home. When Dad pulled our SUV into the driveway, I spotted a big sign hanging from the front porch that read, "Welcome Home, Elder Austin Winchester!" I got out and looked around at the house, Dad's manicured front lawn, and Mom's flower garden. In many ways coming home was like visiting an old friend.

Our neighbor's big ugly dog, Tornado, barked and bared his teeth at me just like before my mission. He was still chained to their big tree in the front yard. I had always believed he'd kill me if he ever broke free. Robbie had been the only one in the neighborhood who could play with Tornado.

Mom had a big dinner ready, and after we'd eaten, I went over to the stake center to meet with our stake president. He interviewed me about my mission, gave me some counsel about education and marriage, and then officially released me. When I got home, I told my mom I was going to take a walk.

"Do you mind if I tag along?" Brianna asked.

"No, not at all."

It took us fifteen minutes to go a block because of all the neighbors who stopped us to welcome me home from my mission. In each case I introduced Brianna as the girl who was waiting for Robbie.

Once we got outside our ward boundaries we were able to make better time.

"You didn't read your mom's letters very closely, did you?" Brianna asked.

"No. How did you know?"

"Robbie can't keep up with them either, so, since your mom sends me a copy, too, I fill him in on the most important things. I could do the same for you now."

"Maybe you'd better."

"Okay, here's what I know. Your Aunt Nancy got married while you were gone. Twice, actually. The last time just a few months ago."

"Twice?"

"Apparently a good man is harder to find than any of us imagined. But the husband she's got now is totally acceptable."

"Anything else I should know?"

"Your dad got downsized. He's now working as a sales representative for a software company."

I shook my head. "Oh, no, I messed up. That's something I should have known."

"It's okay. You were busy. I'll help you catch up."

"Thanks. Oh, I'm sorry I didn't know about you and Robbie."

"It's totally okay. It's strange. You don't know me, but I

feel like I know you. He's often told me what a good influence you were on him. For that I thank you."

"Little Robbie."

"Not anymore."

"You like him a lot, don't you?" I asked.

"Yes, I do. He's always been very considerate of me."

"Actually, come to think of it, I taught him that," I said.

"How?"

"I remember when he was in sixth grade I gave him a gerbil for his birthday. When I found out he wasn't taking good care of it, I went to him and said, 'Robbie, you always need to be thinking, *What can I do for the gerbil today?* You've got to think about the gerbil, not just once in a while, but every day.'" I paused. "You obviously benefitted from Robbie's gerbil experience."

She flashed me a teasing smile. "Are you saying he thinks of me the same way he thought about his gerbil?"

"Yeah, pretty much. Oh, my gosh! He didn't put newspapers on your floor every day, did he?" I asked.

For such a classy looking girl, she had the most amazing laugh. First of all, it was a full-bodied laugh. Every part of her got in on it. To make her laugh became my new goal in life.

"You're way more fun than Robbie," she said. "He's, well, more sincere than funny."

"He learned that from the gerbil. Your average gerbil has a pathetic sense of humor."

We ended up sitting next to each other on two swings in a park. We watched the sunset together. Or, to be more truthful, she watched the sunset, and I watched her. How had Robbie lucked out to have found her?

Even so, I wasn't going to take advantage of her trust in me. I was going to play the part assigned me. I would be the trusted brother.

"We'd better get back," she said. "Your mom and dad will be wondering what happened to us."

It seemed strange, being alone with a girl, after two years of that being against the rules. But it was also . . . good.

"It's been great being with you. I mean, you being a girl, and all."

She laughed for me again. "You are *so* observant!"

"Yes, I am. Except for the color of your eyes. Would you mind if I examined them to determine their exact color?"

"I could just tell you."

"No, that's okay. I'm kind of a hands-on guy."

"Okay, I've got to admit, that worries me just a little," she teased.

"We're talking about eyes here, okay? C'mon, give me a break."

She shrugged. "Okay, be my guest." She opened her eyes wide and leaned slightly toward me.

We made eye contact. It was awesome except for the fact that I got a little distracted. Also, I was taking much more time than one would normally need to determine the color of someone's eyes. And that did make her nervous.

"Let me just tell you, okay?" she said, moving away from me. "My eyes are hazel."

The truth is I didn't know what color hazel was, but I wasn't going to admit that. "Of course they are." I stood up. "Well, let's start back."

As we walked home, I felt a little guilty for having looked into her eyes for so long. I felt as though I needed to explain myself. "I didn't think I'd be this comfortable with a girl right after my mission, but, with you, I am. I guess it's because you're already like a member of the family."

"I feel comfortable with you, too, Austin."

After we got home, we went inside, talked for a while, and then she told us she needed to get back to BYU. I have to admit, I wasn't that thrilled about her leaving. I walked her out to her car and thanked her for coming to the airport to welcome me home.

"In about a year, I'll be welcoming Robbie home. I can hardly wait."

"Yeah, well, he's a lucky guy. I'll say that for him."

"I'll see you Saturday afternoon, okay?" she said and then got into her car, flashed me that great smile, and drove off.

The next day my dad took me fishing. Not because I'm that much into it but because he is. But it did give us a chance to talk.

He asked about my plans. I shrugged. "I don't know. Work this summer and start school in the fall. That's about it."

He told me about his new job, and he asked me some questions about my mission. So it was good to be together, even though we didn't catch any fish.

When I woke up Friday morning, I stayed in bed for a little while, just thinking. It seemed strange not to have a companion to worry about, and I even felt a little guilty, like there was something I should be doing.

My mom took care of that, and the day was taken up working for her around the house, weeding our garden, and mowing the lawn. The reason for all this cleaning was that we were having people over Sunday after church, and she wanted everything in good shape. That much hadn't changed. She had always been a neat freak about our house and yard.

She even asked me to clean the garage, too, but with everything else she had me doing, I didn't have time to get to that. Besides, it wasn't a project that I could do by myself. For every item I picked up I'd have had to ask her what to do with it. And what guy wants that much supervision from his mom? Not me.

Brianna came for dinner Saturday and then stayed the night. I confess, she was even better-looking than I remembered, if that's possible. Knowing that she was my brother's girlfriend made it a little awkward to be around her, and I still felt guilty for having used some lame excuse to look into her eyes. So at first I backed off and tried to stay out of her way.

That night Brianna was staying in the guest room, directly over my head in my downstairs bedroom. I couldn't get to sleep right away because I could hear her walking around above me, and I kept wondering what she was doing. It wasn't until it was quiet above me that I eventually dozed off.

I got up at seven and went into the kitchen to work on my talk. Brianna was already up, sitting at the kitchen table reading the scriptures, wearing a pair of olive green flannel pajamas and a robe.

"Good morning," she said.

I was noticing her eyes. They looked green to me. "Uh, good morning. Did you sleep well?" I asked.

"Yes, and you?"

"Not really."

"How come?" she asked.

"I'm having a little trouble adjusting. Basically, I want to go back on my mission for another couple of years."

"What do you miss the most?"

"The people."

"Yes, of course. I'm sure they're missing you, too."

"I feel like there's nothing in my life that will ever compare to my mission."

"I can see why you'd feel like that now. Tell me about the people you taught."

It took nearly an hour. Me talking while we had some cereal and toast. And then it was time to get ready for church.

"I'm still not sure what to talk about," I said.

"I think you've just given me your talk. People love to hear missionaries tell about their experiences, and the people they met."

"You think so?"

"Definitely. That and your testimony."

"Okay, maybe I'll do that. Thanks."

During my talk, I kept looking down in the audience at Brianna, who nodded approval that I was on the right track.

After sacrament meeting she came up to me and shook my hand. "You did a fantastic job!"

"Thanks."

As she was telling me in detail what she liked about what I'd said, I noticed that our handshake, which had begun appropriately, was fast becoming questionable because we had quit moving our hands up and down, but we still had hand contact.

When she finally noticed the problem, she let go and pulled away.

Now I really was embarrassed. I'd forgotten I was holding her hand, that's all. It could happen to anyone. But it needed to be addressed. "I shook your hand too long, didn't I? Sorry."

She got a thoughtful look on her face and pretended to be approaching this from a referee's point of view. "Actually, there is no rule about the duration of a handshake. Where we went wrong, I believe, is we failed to keep our hands in motion. As I understand the official rules, as long as the hands are moving, it constitutes a legitimate handshake."

All I'd ever wanted from life was a girl who would be whimsical with me. Like what we were doing right then.

"So, what you're saying is, if the hands are moving, it's not a violation, right?" I said.

She nodded. "It makes sense, really. I mean, think about it. There is no such thing as a 'hand-still,' right?" she said.

"I suppose that would technically be called holding hands."

"I believe you're correct on that."

She was amazing. She had a way of holding her eyes wide open as she considered something, and there was a bit of a tease in her. I did notice that her eyes now looked brown to me.

I wanted to tell her how much fun I was having, and how gorgeous she was, but, because of Robbie, I didn't say anything.

On the other hand, I did feel a little guilty that I'd held

hands with the girl who was waiting for my brother, even if it was only for like maybe twenty seconds beyond what most people would consider appropriate.

I stayed in the chapel talking to ward members until they all went to Sunday School and then our family went home to get ready for a luncheon we were having for relatives, friends, and neighbors.

My mom asked Brianna and me to set up chairs and banquet tables in the backyard and then to set the table.

"There won't be as many here as there were for my farewell," I said.

"Why's that?"

"Most of the girls from high school who adored me got married while I was gone. Apparently they didn't adore me two years' worth."

"Did you have a girl waiting for you?" Brianna asked.

"Yeah, more or less, I guess. She got married about six months ago."

"Her loss, right?" she said with one of her dazzling smiles.

"We can always think so. Do you think you'll wait until Robbie comes home?"

"Oh, I know I will. There's absolutely no doubt about that."

I was surprised at her answer because she said it with such certainty.

"How do you know you'll wait?"

"Because people all the time are telling me I won't make it for two years. I don't like being told I'm not going to achieve my goals. So I'm going to prove them all wrong."

"Well, if it ever gets hard for you, give me a call, and I'll come over and tell you what a great guy he is."

"That's a good idea. Sometimes lately, I've had trouble remembering what he was like."

"I'll get hold of some of our family pictures so you'll know how he was as he was growing up," I said.

"Great idea."

"And if there were certain places you guys used to go or special memories you have of him, you and I could go there and relive those memories."

She considered that for a moment, her eyes wide open. "Hmm. Do you think that would really help?" That's not necessarily why I had suggested it, but I was glad she would even think about it.

By the time we finished our work, some people had arrived so I spent my time talking with them. Brianna made herself useful by helping my mom.

An hour later Brianna came up to me. "Hey, Austin. I'm going now. It was fun to see you again. Great talk."

"Thanks, but do you really have to go now?"

She pulled a face. "Yeah, I do. I usually don't like to study on Sundays, but I've got a paper due tomorrow."

"Well, can I walk you out to your car?"

"Sure."

"I'll be at BYU fall semester," I said. "Is it okay if I call you once in a while?" I asked.

"Please do. Anytime." She gave me her number, got in her car, gave me a wave, and drove away.

I stood there on the curb, watching her drive down our street, wondering how my big oaf of a brother had gotten so lucky as to find a girl like her.

The next Sunday, in my home ward, our elders quorum president announced a stake softball league and asked how many of us could play. I raised my hand, but when I found out that all the games were on Tuesday nights, I had to cancel. I'd gotten a job working part-time for a trucking company, handling freight at night, and Tuesday was one of my shifts. After priesthood, one of the guys in the quorum said he wanted to play but didn't have a baseball glove. He asked if he could borrow mine.

"Well, actually, I was going to use my brother's glove, but I guess you can use it."

Robbie had been a star on his high school baseball team, helping them win the state championship his senior year.

My friend dropped by that afternoon and picked it up.

Because it wasn't actually my glove, I wrote Robbie a letter asking if it would be okay to use it. I didn't mention that I was going to loan it out, but it would probably be several weeks before he answered me, and besides, I was sure he'd say yes.

Three weeks later I got a letter from Robbie saying I could use his baseball glove but only if I didn't use it for softball. He explained that because a softball is so much bigger than a baseball it would wreck the pocket in the glove. He told me he planned to try to play baseball in college when he got back and would need it then. Oh, and he also told me not to loan it to anyone.

By that time, though, the season was almost over, and I decided to let my friend continue to use the glove. I knew how busy Robbie was as a missionary. I didn't want to distract him from missionary work by writing to let him know I'd actually loaned his glove for softball. *Maybe he'll be so spiritual when he comes home from his mission, he won't even care,* I thought. *After all, the gospel is more important than some dumb baseball glove.*

By the first week in August, softball had ended. In priesthood I asked the guy who'd borrowed Robbie's mitt to bring it next Sunday. He promised he would, but he kept forgetting.

The Sunday before I was to leave for BYU, he told me he had dropped it by the house during the week. "Nobody was home but the garage door was open so I just put it in there."

Of course I should have gone out to the garage after I got home from church and returned it to Robbie's room, but I didn't do that. Who would have ever thought that would be important some day?

I didn't have any further contact with Brianna until I showed up at BYU for fall semester. A few days after classes started, we saw each other on campus and stopped to talk. I asked if I could walk her to her apartment. She seemed happy for the company. I certainly was. I'd actually forgotten how much fun it was to be with her.

"Be honest with me, okay? Do you like your roommates?" she asked.

"I've never even thought about it. We don't see each other that much."

She sighed. "That is what is so great about guys! Guys don't even try to be close to their roommates. You're lucky you don't have to live in an apartment full of girls. It's like high drama from day one."

"In what way?"

"On the first day we were all together, one of the girls insisted on a meeting to determine where each of us was going to put our food in the refrigerator. That meeting like dragged on for forty-five minutes. One girl didn't want to have the upper right part of the shelf because she was afraid her milk would freeze. Two girls insisted on being on the lower shelf in the center. We were almost to an agreement when one girl, who'd been quiet most of the time, got all teary-eyed and said it's not fair. So we had to start all over again."

"Are you serious? Guys don't talk about things like that. Like in the morning, you see a roommate, and you say, 'How's it goin'?' And he says, 'Can't complain.' And then basically you're done for the entire day as far as roommates go."

"What's the Guy Rule for food in the refrigerator?" she asked.

"You can eat or drink anything in there, whether it belongs to you or not, but there's just one rule: You can't take it *all*. So you've got to be careful. Like if I'm going to use a roommate's milk, I can't use so much that he'll be out of milk for breakfast. If I need more than what I can safely take from him, I take some from another roommate's carton."

She laughed. "That is so reasonable! Can I move in with you?"

"Yeah, sure, no problem. Bring plenty of milk though because I'm never going to actually buy any myself."

Gosh, I loved her laugh. For someone that beautiful to belt out a laugh because of something I'd said was for me like the highlight of my life.

"What if one of your roommates is going on a date?" she continued. "Does he keep telling you over and over again how excited he is and then ask your advice, like every five minutes, about what he should wear?"

"No, a guy roommate will never even tell us he's going on a date. He'll just leave. He'll be gone three or four hours and then he'll come back and go to bed. He doesn't tell us how it went and we don't ask. The truth is, we don't really care."

She raised both hands high in the air. "Yes! That's how it should be! Why do each of my roommates think they have to tell me everything? Why do I have to be shown three possible variations of what she might wear and then be asked to decide? Why do I have to be told in detail what the guy said when he asked her out? And after it's over, when I just want to go to sleep, why do I have to be told everything that happened on her stupid date? I don't want to know! I just want to be left alone!"

"You know what? You would fit in so well with guys."

"I know. I totally would. But that's not the worst. The thing I dread the most is the weekends. Each of my roommates is seeing someone, so they'll all go on dates, and I'll be left all alone in the apartment with only my 8 x 10 picture of Robbie. Actually, it's his high school graduation picture. I keep getting older, but he stays the same."

She paused as though she weren't sure she should say what she was thinking. "You want to know something weird? Last week I realized I was starting to think of him as my nephew."

That seemed like an odd thing to say, but it also made me very happy. "If you get lonely on the weekends, give me a call. I'll never be doing anything."

She hesitated and then asked, "Are you serious?"

"Totally."

"Well, actually, I will be lonely this Friday night."

"Okay, I'll come over. What time?"

"I'd say eight-thirty. By then all my roommates will be gone. I don't want to have to explain you to them."

"What do you want to do when we're together?" I asked.

She thought about it for a while and then said, "I think we should take a walk."

"Yeah, sure, we'll totally do that. Then we don't have to explain anything to anybody. Some people don't have cars so they have to walk all the time. Sometimes they even walk together with a friend. Nobody in the world would confuse taking a walk with being on a date."

She nodded. "Exactly."

Chapter Two

Friday night was a perfect fall evening with a full moon, and we walked until nearly one o'clock in the morning. Okay, not the whole time. We stopped in at the Wilkinson Center and watched people dance. Oh, and, also, we danced for a while, too. And then we had ice cream.

She was wearing a tan sweater over a white shirt. Her eyes now looked brown.

As we were about to leave the Wilkinson Center, I stopped her. "I'm still not sure what color your eyes are."

"Hazel."

"I have no idea what that means."

"Okay, this is your last chance. If you don't get it this time, you can look it up on Wikipedia."

"Let's find a place where there's good lighting," I said.

We found a place. "Could you just lean up against the wall? This won't take long."

I leaned toward her and, once again, we made eye contact.

"What do you see?" she asked.

"There's some green, and some brown, and some gold."

"That's what people mean when they say hazel eyes," she said.

"Oh, I didn't know that."

We continued looking into each other's eyes until we heard someone coming down the hall. And then she kind of panicked. "If one of my roommates sees us together, I'll be answering their questions all night."

"My examination is done."

"Your examination?"

"I just needed to know, that's all."

"Yeah, yeah," she said.

We bought four oranges at a grocery store, and I tried to teach her how to juggle. The only problem was I didn't know how to juggle either. We ended up eating the oranges we'd ruined by dropping them so much. Oh, and we laughed a lot.

And of course we talked. I learned all about her. She's from Fillmore, Utah. She has two older sisters who are married and have kids. She also told me about her younger brother, Todd, who was in his senior year.

"This has been the best Friday night I've had since Robbie left," she said as we walked back to her apartment. "I'm not a bit depressed. Thank you so much!"

Before she went inside, she gave me a big hug. I held on just to prolong the experience for her because I figured that with Robbie gone for over a year, she might be possibly hug-deprived.

"It was fun for me, too," I said, reluctantly releasing her.

"This is the most time I've spent with a girl since my senior prom. Do you think we can do it again sometime?"

She paused. "Well, actually, I get depressed Saturday nights, too."

"Yeah, sure, no problem. I'll come over tomorrow night."

"You sure?"

"Why not? You're the only girl I know on campus."

"I'll introduce you to some girls in my ward," she said.

"No, that's okay. Well, I'd better be going."

She gave me another hug. "Robbie will be so grateful to you for what you're doing."

It was probably bad timing for her to mention Robbie when we were hugging. "You think so?"

"Oh, yes. He's lucky to have such a great brother."

That caused me sufficient guilt to make me pull away from her. "What we did tonight is okay, right?" I asked. "I mean, in terms of Robbie."

"Yeah, it is. It's fine. You've spared me a miserable evening. Thanks so much."

I didn't get much sleep that night. I knew this could turn awkward, Robbie being my brother and all. And her being drop-dead gorgeous and, my gosh, so much fun to be with.

I spent most of Saturday studying. That night, I went over to Brianna's apartment at about eight o'clock. While I was waiting for someone to answer my knock, the door opened and one of her roommates and her date walked out past me.

"Is Brianna here?" I asked.

"Yeah, she is," the girl said. "I'm Lisa, who are you?"

"Uh. Austin. Brianna's my brother's girlfriend." I don't

20

know why I felt as though I had to say that. Maybe I was feeling a little bit guilty, after all.

Just then, Brianna came to the door, and the couple left.

"Hi," Brianna said. "Sorry, I didn't hear you knock." She'd pulled her hair back into a little different style and was wearing a dark blue BYU sweatshirt and jeans. Once again, she looked great.

"Would you like to come in?" she asked, holding the door open.

"Well, uh, no. I mean, I thought maybe you'd like to go somewhere. Maybe get something to eat."

"That'd be good. What did you have in mind?"

"How about pizza?"

"Sure," she replied. "That sounds great."

We ended up at the Brick Oven in Provo where we sat talking, long after our pizza and drinks were gone. She told me more about her family and what it had been like, growing up in Fillmore, and I was mostly content to just listen to her and watch her while she talked. She had an amazing face, but the thing is, she didn't seem to know it.

By the time we walked back up the hill, it was almost midnight, but we still stood on the porch outside her apartment and talked for another hour before she said she needed to get to bed.

On my walk home, I realized Robbie's name hadn't come up all evening.

When I first woke up on Sunday morning, I thought about attending her campus ward, but then I decided that would be a mistake because there might be people in her ward who knew Robbie and so they'd be wondering what was going on. And who knew what her roommates would say if they found out we were friends. So I went to my own ward.

On Monday, Brianna texted me to say she wanted to bring me lunch after one of my classes. We ate it on a bench outside the library. And then we took a walk around campus. On our walk we met a friend of hers who had been her roommate when she was dating Robbie.

"This is Robbie's brother, Austin," Brianna said. "We get together once in a while and talk about my favorite topic."

"Which is Robbie, right?" the girl asked, lifting an eyebrow.

"That's right. Today he's filling me in on the cute things Robbie did when he was a boy."

"How fun! Good to meet you, Austin." She gave Brianna a quizzical glance and walked away.

I think we both felt a little uncomfortable, since we hadn't actually been talking about Robbie. In fact, we had both pretty much avoided talking about him.

"Is that okay what I said?" she asked.

"Oh, yeah, sure. It was totally okay."

"Good."

She stopped. "Look, I think I need to say something."

"Okay."

"In some ways this is turning out a little different than I thought it would," she said. "Well, the thing is, I'm actually enjoying being with you."

"Yeah, me too. So how do you want to handle this?"

"I think it's probably better if we don't hug each other . . . too much," she said.

"Just a few occasional hugs, though, right?" I asked.

"Yes, I think hugging is okay . . . Just not too much . . . or too long . . . or too close."

"Oh, I totally agree. How about if I hug you like only every other time I think about it."

"Thank you." She opened her eyes wide and then asked, "Uh, how often do you think about it?"

The correct answer was like every two or three minutes, but there was no way I was going to tell her that. "Actually, not that often. You know, just once in a while. Oh, also, just for the record, I would assume that kissing would be totally out of the question for us, right?" I asked.

"Oh, yes, totally."

"I knew that. I just wanted, you know, for us to have discussed it, so we're both on the same page."

"I agree. It's good to set down ground rules for things like this."

"Is there anything else we should talk about?" I asked.

"Well, actually, there is one other thing I've been wanting to talk to you about. I play the harp."

"That's okay. It's nothing to be ashamed of," I teased.

She faked being mad at me. "Watch it, fella! I don't need intervention, okay?"

"So why are you bringing this up?"

"Would you like to know the worst thing about playing the harp?"

"Yes, I would."

"Hauling it around from place to place."

"Oh, sure. Look, if you ever need any help hauling it, let me know. I can put it in the back of my pickup."

"You have a pickup? How come I've never seen it?"

"Because it's in such bad shape. It belonged to my

grandfather. It's thirty years old, and it needs a paint job, but, hey, at least it runs. It's certainly good enough to haul a harp."

"You wouldn't mind doing that for me?" she asked.

"No, but the harp might complain being in such a ghetto truck."

She laughed. "It's such a pain to transport it in my Honda, with part of it sticking out the back."

"Where do you need to take it?"

She hesitated before answering, then said, "If you're serious about helping me, I could use you this Friday. A friend of mine from high school plays the flute. Her name is Sophie, and we play at wedding receptions. We're playing at one on Friday night in Draper. We'd need to leave at about five-thirty to get there on time and get set up. Would it be too much to ask if you could drive us up there in your pickup and then bring us back after we're done?"

"No problem. I'll need to figure out how to secure it, though, but I think I can do that."

She reached for my hand. "Austin, you're the best! Thank you so much!"

"Glad to help out."

I looked down at our hands. They weren't moving, so you couldn't really get away with saying it was just a hand-shake. To buy some time, I moved our hands up and down, but the repetition rate was way too slow.

She looked down at our hands and sighed.

"Look, let's just be honest with each other, okay?" I said.

She winced and closed her eyes. "Okay, I guess."

"I think what's happening here is that Robbie has been

gone for so long and that you're really beginning to miss the physical contact you had with him. Like hugging."

She sighed and then nodded. "You're right. It's been more than a year for me, you know, to hug and be hugged. And what do I get in place of that? Some stupid letter once a week! And the thing is, all he writes about is missionary work. You think that does me any good?"

"What would you think if I became a safe alternative for you in the hugging department?"

"What are we talking about?" she asked.

"Just friendly hugs. Never any kissing, though. That wouldn't be right."

"Why would you do this for me?"

I tried my best to sound noble. "Hey, Robbie would do the same for me."

"You think so?"

"Absolutely." I had trouble keeping a straight face.

I expected her to start laughing and playfully punch me in the chest and tell me, "Nice try!" But she didn't. That meant she trusted me to be true to my brother. Which was, in a way, crazy. Robbie and I had never been that close.

We were both embarrassed about the entire discussion, but we assured each other that we shouldn't feel guilty about an occasional hug, like once or twice a week. Only as friends of course.

On Wednesday after classes, I dropped by her apartment to take a look at her harp and figure out a way to secure it in the back of my pickup. The one good thing is that she had a dolly so I didn't have to drag it around. She also had a covering on her harp to protect it from the elements.

I rolled her harp out the door and up a ramp I'd made

from a couple of two-by-fours and a piece of plywood. Under Brianna's close supervision, I gently lowered the harp down on its side, resting it on foam padding that now covered the bed of the pickup. And then I started working on figuring out how to secure it, using a bunch of bungee cords. She watched for a while and then got bored and went inside.

When I was done, I rang her doorbell. "Come see what I did," I said.

Outside again, I showed her what I'd come up with. "I think that will keep it secure," I said.

"Wow! Good job!" She gave me a hug. "That's perfect!"

"You know me. I'm always glad to help out." For Robbie's sake, I let her hug me as long as she wanted. Which wasn't nearly long enough for me.

On Friday afternoon at five o'clock, I dropped by Brianna's apartment and rolled her harp out to the pickup and secured it. It wasn't just the harp, either. On other trips, I carried her stool, a music stand, a bag of strings, and her music. And then we drove over to pick up Sophie.

Brianna slid over next to me and Sophie sat next to the door. She was a quiet girl with amazing cheekbones. Her beautiful dark brown hair was totally corralled in though, pulled into a tight bun, like a librarian might do. Also, she seemed a little sad. I couldn't tell if it was because she had to ride in my old Chevy pickup or if it was deeper than that.

"Tell me about yourself, Sophie," I said as we were driving.

She turned her head away from me. "There's not much to tell."

"I'm sure that's not true. Where are you from?"

"Fillmore, Utah. Brianna comes from there, too."

"Yeah, I know. What's great about coming from Fillmore?" I asked.

Sophie wouldn't look at me. "I don't know."

"How big is your family?"

"I have an older brother. He's in jail, though."

"Oh, that's too bad."

"Not really. He deserved to be sent there."

I was running out of things to ask her. "Tell me about your mom and dad."

"We don't know where my dad is."

"Oh. How long has he been away?" I asked.

"Since I was ten years old."

"Oh, that's a long time."

"I don't miss him."

"Wasn't he a very good dad?" I asked.

She shook her head. "No."

"So, after your dad left, everything depended on your mom?" I asked.

"Yes."

"Does she work?"

"Yes. She's the school librarian in our high school."

That answered the question about her hair being in a bun. "Good for her. When did you start playing the flute?"

"Sixth grade. I took lessons."

"Terrific. And now look at you. Now you're playing for weddings. That's great you can do that."

She shrugged. "I need the money. Real bad. I work in food service in the mornings, too."

"Your mom must be very proud of you."

She permitted herself a brief, weak smile. "I think she

27

is. But I'm the lucky one. I don't know what I'd do without her."

"I'm honored to get to know more about you."

She seemed surprised I'd say that. "Oh."

A few minutes later we pulled up to the ward building where the reception was to be held.

I had Brianna and Sophie go in and scout out the cultural hall where they'd be playing while I was unloading the harp.

As I approached the entry to the building, Brianna was there to open the door for me.

"Thank you for being so kind to Sophie," she said. "Sometimes guys ignore her."

"Hey, I enjoyed talking to her."

"I could tell you did." I was balancing the harp and rolling it toward the cultural hall door when Brianna called my name.

"What?"

"You're one of the nicest, most considerate guys I've ever known."

"Thanks. It's all about the gerbil, right?"

"No, it isn't. It's all about you."

That sounded suspiciously like a compliment to me, and it made me happy.

Once I got the girls set up, I went out to my pickup, grabbed a garment bag with my suit, white shirt, and tie, and went into the men's restroom to change. I didn't want to look out of place at the reception.

I offered to get the girls something to eat before the reception started and left to find a fast-food place. When I got back, the three of us ate in one of the classrooms.

"Sophie, tell Austin about your application to Julliard," Brianna said.

Sophie avoided eye contact and was staring at the wall behind me. "I was a finalist for a scholarship to Julliard School of Music in New York City."

"Isn't that great?" Brianna said.

"Yeah, it is! Totally!" I practically shouted. Still, I was confused. "So why are you here at BYU?"

"I didn't actually win the scholarship. I was just one of ten finalists."

Brianna jumped in with positive guns blazing. "But think about it! How many people are among the top ten finalists for a flute scholarship at Julliard?"

"Ten?" I asked, wondering if it was a trick question.

"Yes, but that's like ten in the entire United States. That makes Sophie one of the best young flutists in the world today!"

"Yeah, that's amazing!" I said. "Exceptional is what it is! You should be proud."

Sophie looked as though she were going to cry. "If I had actually received the scholarship, I wouldn't be here now."

"Where would you be?" I asked.

"At Julliard," she said.

"You know what? If you think about it, that really stands to reason," I said.

Icy cold silence. And then Sophie wiped at her eyes and asked to be excused and left the room.

After she was gone, Brianna said, "She's usually a lot of fun."

"You know what? I can totally tell that."

"Oh, also, besides the flute going for her, she has what I would call a perfect nose. You should ask her out," she said.

"Why?"

"Don't you like her nose?" Brianna asked.

"You want me to ask her out because of her nose?" I asked.

"It's a very good nose. Don't say it isn't."

"Okay, I agree with you about her nose. Her cheekbones are good too."

"So, will you ask her out?" she asked me.

"Actually, if you want to know the truth, I don't see myself asking a girl out just because of her nose, even if you throw in her cheekbones to sweeten the deal."

"Why not? That's what guys do, isn't it? Fixate on some part of a girl's anatomy."

I cleared my throat. "I'm sorry to be the one to break this to you, but it's not usually the nose."

"Yeah, yeah, I know," she said with some resentment in her voice. "Well, her face is good too."

"Yes, it is, I agree. It's a good face. Great symmetry."

"So, you'll ask her out, right?" she asked.

"No way. Not if it's just her and me," I said.

"Why not?"

"I wouldn't know what to talk about. What if I say something, and she bursts out crying?"

"You can always ask her about her mom. She has an amazing mom."

"In what way?" I asked.

"Her mom is a world-famous librarian."

"You're totally making that up, aren't you?" I asked.

"No, I'm serious."

"I don't believe you. I mean, how does a librarian from Fillmore, Utah, become world-famous?"

"She actually invented a way to improve the Dewey Decimal System."

I tried not to laugh, but I couldn't help myself.

Brianna stood up and put her hands on her hips, a gesture used by every grade school teacher I'd ever had. "You think the Dewey Decimal System is trivial? Well, let me tell you something, buddy-boy, it is not. It is a very valuable tool that helps millions of library patrons every day find what they want in the library. To me that says only one thing: Dewey Decimal was a genius."

I started laughing so hard I slid off my chair onto the floor.

"What?" she asked.

"You think that *Decimal* was his last name?" I gasped.

She realized her mistake and pursed her lips.

I was still on the floor laughing my head off.

And then Sophie came back into the room.

Brianna quickly came over to me and put her hand on my shoulder. "There, there, Austin, it will be okay. Don't cry."

I took the hint and put my hand over my eyes. I didn't stop laughing, but sometimes a good laugh can be mistaken for sobbing.

"What's wrong?" Sophie asked.

"Austin was just telling me how his gerbil died. Even though it happened years ago, he's still mourning the loss."

"Oh, I'm sorry. How did it die?"

"It hid in the dirty clothes hamper," Brianna said. "And

when Austin's mom did a wash, it got dumped in there by mistake."

Sophie patted me on the head. "I'm sorry."

I nodded, stifling my fake sobs.

"The guests are beginning to arrive," Sophie said to Brianna. "So we should start."

"I'll be there in a minute."

Sophie left.

I stood up.

Brianna and I looked at each other but didn't say anything. I'm not sure what we would have said.

"I'd better go," she said.

She took three steps and then stopped and turned around. "My main weakness is trying to make everything turn out well for everyone. So that everyone's happy. You know, like I did for Sophie so she wouldn't know we were laughing at her mom's expense. I do that, you know."

"Me, too, except maybe I haven't had as much experience as you have."

"We'll talk," she said.

"Yeah, some day. Maybe. No hurry, though, right?"

She looked at me for a long time, sighed, and then left the room.

Funny thing though, I knew what she meant by her sigh.

Chapter Three

For the next two and a half hours I sat in the corner of the cultural hall and compared Brianna with every other girl there. There were two or three that had her beat in some random category but none that were more engaging, more open, or friendlier. For instance, when someone walked up to her to request a song, her smile and her eyes made it clear that she valued that person. She treated everyone with respect. Even the jerk who said he couldn't understand why anyone would book a harp and a flute player for a wedding. "For a funeral maybe, but not for a wedding."

Actually, they played beautifully together. Sophie really was an exceptional musician. But it was Brianna who captured my attention. I couldn't keep my eyes off her. The graceful way she used her hands was fascinating. She was really into her music and had this dream-like look on her face as she played.

After an hour I took Brianna and Sophie some ice water and a small cookie. Brianna smiled and placed her hand on my arm. "Oh, this is great! How did you know this is exactly what I needed?"

"Yeah, thanks," Sophie said with no real enthusiasm in her voice. She drank the water but set the cookie down on her flute case.

Because I didn't know anyone there, I was mostly ignored, which gave me the freedom to watch the guests and listen in on their conversations.

Like the husband and wife who arrived much later than most of the other guests.

"We're lucky we even got here," the wife complained. "Why don't you ever stop and ask for directions?"

"You're blaming me for being late? I had to wait half an hour for you to get ready. And for what? Do you really think anyone cares what you've done with your hair?"

"Well, I know you don't care," she retorted. "Not anymore anyway."

"Are you ever going to stop throwing that in my face? It was just one lunch, and she's my secretary, for crying out loud."

And then they noticed me. "Hi, folks, welcome to the Fielding/Hansen reception," I said warmly, as if this were part of my official duties.

Of course I was curious about the 'just one lunch.' But I didn't figure I was going to find out about that. But, still, it was strange. They were married. They lived in the same house. They slept in the same bed. If this was wedded bliss, I wanted no part of it.

She was worried that he was more interested in his secretary than he was in her. He suspected she purposely took more time to get ready just to make him mad. So how long had this quiet war been going on?

Just before the reception was to end, I was standing outside in the dark next to my pickup when a guy and a girl walked to the car next to me. They apparently didn't see me.

"What about tonight?" he asked.

"What about it?"

"You remember what we talked about last time, about us taking our relationship to a new level? I think we're both ready."

She shook her head. "Like I said before, I'm not ready."

"Why not? You know I care about you, right?"

"We haven't been seeing each other that long."

"It'd be a great way to celebrate me getting a raise."

"A great way for you, maybe."

"You think I only want this for me?"

She looked directly at him. "Yes, Josh, that's exactly what I think."

And then they got into his car and drove off.

You can learn a lot by spending time at a wedding reception, just watching and listening.

A few minutes later, Brianna came out and told me they were done. I went inside and hauled everything out to my pickup and rigged it up.

As we pulled out of the parking lot and onto the street, I said, "You two have worked so hard. Let me take you out for something to eat."

"That sounds good to me. Sophie, what do you think?"

"Okay," she said. "Can I go change first? I don't want to spill anything on this dress."

"Yeah, sure, maybe we should all change," Brianna suggested.

Once we got back to Provo, we dropped Sophie off first and waited in my pickup for her to change. While we were waiting, Brianna moved closer to me, found my hand, held it, and squeezed.

"Is that so I won't fall asleep?" I asked.

"No, it's to thank you for being so good to Sophie. She was my best friend in high school, so I've known her a long time. And she usually doesn't like being around guys."

"How come?"

"She's terrified of them. She had a bad experience with a guy when she was in eighth grade."

"I'm sorry."

"Yeah, me, too. She won't talk about it."

"How do you know about it then?"

"The guy who did it to her told all his friends. So everyone in school knew about it. And that traumatized her even more."

"If guys only knew the damage they do when they mistreat a girl," I said.

"A guy like that jerk wouldn't care."

"He might if someone explained it to him," I said.

"I don't believe that. Guys like him only want to take. Never to give."

"You're probably right."

We were still holding hands. "Can I ask a question?" I asked. "Would you characterize what we're doing now as shaking hands or holding hands?"

She quickly pulled her hand away. "Sorry."

"It's okay."

"I just wanted you to know I appreciate you paying attention to Sophie."

"Maybe we should go out for something to eat every time after you and Sophie play for a reception," I said. "You know, for her sake, to help her feel more comfortable around a guy."

"That would be great! Especially for Sophie."

"I agree. This is all about Sophie."

Sophie came back wearing a Sunday dress.

"You look great, Sophie!" Brianna cheered.

"This can be washed," she said.

"You're a beautiful and talented girl, Sophie," I said.

"Not really."

"Well, I think you are," I said.

"I do, too," Brianna said. "You know what? Instead of Austin and me changing too, maybe we should just drop off my harp and everything else at my apartment, then go to the place where we're going to eat."

We ended up at a restaurant known for its pies. We ordered and then Brianna excused herself to use the restroom.

Sophie looked around at all the people around us. "If someone came in now and looked at us, they would think that you and I were on a date," she said quietly.

"I think you're right about that."

"I've never been on a date," she said, looking down at her water glass.

"Not ever?"

"Not ever, but I've thought about it."

"Would you go on a date with me if I asked you?" I asked.

She got a deer-in-the-headlight look on her face. "I don't know."

"Well, think about it."

"You'd never ask me."

"Why do you say that?"

"Because you like Brianna."

"Brianna is waiting for my brother to come home from his mission."

"I know, but you two like each other."

"Of course we do, but only as friends."

"I've never had a friend who was a boy."

"Well, now you've got me. I'll be your friend."

She lowered her head. "Don't say it if you don't mean it."

"I mean it. I'll be Brianna's friend, and I'll be your friend, too."

She closed her eyes. Tears began to slide down her cheeks.

I wanted her to know I cared about her. "Sophie, would it be all right with you if I held your hand for just a minute?" I asked.

She didn't answer, but I took her hand, anyway. But, still, she kept crying.

I patted her hand. "It's going to be okay. Brianna and I are your friends, and we care about you."

Brianna returned to her seat, looked over at Sophie in tears and me holding her hand. "Is something wrong?" she asked.

"I just told Sophie I wanted to be her friend."

"I'm glad for you, Sophie. Austin is a great friend for any girl to have."

Sophie asked if we could eat the pie some place where we would be alone. So when the waitress brought our order, I asked if she could box it up for us and give us some napkins and forks. A short time later, I paid the bill and we left.

Sophie didn't want to go back to her apartment, so I drove up Provo Canyon, found a side road and took it, went a few miles, and then turned off onto another road and parked. It was an isolated place, and when I turned off the engine and the lights, it was really dark.

"I need to talk to Brianna," Sophie said.

"Right. I'll get out and leave you two alone," I said.

I walked a short distance, found a fallen tree stump to sit on, and waited.

In the beginning I couldn't hear what they were saying, but a little later I could hear Sophie sobbing and Brianna trying to console her, and then it went back to them talking again.

An hour later Brianna called me back to my pickup. "Sophie wants to go out with you, but she wants you to promise that you won't hurt her."

"I promise I won't hurt you, Sophie."

"Okay," she said in her little-girl voice.

"She and I need to talk some more," Brianna said to me.

"Is it okay if I get something? It's on Sophie's side."

"Sure."

Sophie opened the door on her side. I reached into the glove compartment and grabbed the harmonica my grandfather had given me when I was a boy. "You girls gave me a concert tonight, so now I'll give you one."

"Well, that sounds fun. Doesn't it, Sophie?"

She didn't say anything but nodded her head yes.

I returned to my tree stump, sat down, and began trying to remember the songs my grandfather had taught me.

A half hour later, Brianna called to me. "I think we're ready to eat pie now," she said.

"Okay, great."

"Thanks for the harmonica concert. We should have you play a couple of songs sometime at a wedding reception," Brianna said.

"Forget it. People at wedding receptions do not want amateur night."

"You've been a real help to Sophie tonight, hasn't he, Sophie?"

Sophie didn't answer but did nod her head slightly. She was sitting with her hands folded together in her lap with her head sort of bowed, looking down.

"I just asked her for a date. That was easy."

"Thank you," Sophie said quietly.

"I'm the lucky one."

I found a radio station that played country music, and we stood next to the hood of the truck, eating pie and singing along to the music. At least, Brianna and I sang along. After a while, Sophie said she was scared of the dark so I turned on the headlights, which seemed to make her feel better.

We traded bites of pie so we all got to taste what the other two had ordered.

When we finished eating and were about to get back into the truck, Brianna suggested we have a group hug, but Sophie said she wasn't ready for that. She did say she had enjoyed being with us. "Very much," she said, staring at the ground.

And then we started back. When we got into town, I

dropped Sophie off first so she wouldn't freak out about having to be alone with me. At Brianna's place, she helped me move everything inside her apartment, and then I left.

Half an hour later, just before going to bed, my cell phone rang. I picked up. It was Brianna.

"After you dropped me off, Sophie called. She's freaking out about being alone with you on a date. So I drove over to her apartment, and I'm with her now. Can I ask you some of the questions she asked me about your date with her?"

"Okay."

"You won't force her into your bedroom, will you?" Brianna asked me.

"Let me talk to her," I said.

It took Brianna a while to get Sophie to agree to talk with me.

"Hello?"

"Hi, Sophie. Brianna said you have some questions."

"I'm so sorry to bother you."

"Hey, don't worry about it. I never go to sleep before one in the morning anyway." I felt pretty awkward and didn't know exactly what to say. But I took a deep breath and said, "Brianna says you're worried about me forcing you into my bedroom. I promise you, I would never do that."

"Okay. I think I knew that, but I just wanted you to tell me."

"What other questions do you have for me?"

"You won't do . . . bad things to me, will you?"

"No. That's something I would never do."

"I'm not sure I can be with you without Brianna."

"It's no problem. We can take Brianna, too."

"But then it wouldn't be a date."

"What if we totally ignore her and pretend she's not even there?"

At first I thought Sophie was crying, but then I realized she was giggling. I could hear her say to Brianna, "If we bring you with us, Austin says we're going to totally ignore you."

"That's okay. I can just be in the background, you know, just so you feel safe."

Sophie came back on the line. "That sounds okay. I'm sure you're a nice guy and everything, but I just need some time to get used to this."

"Absolutely. We'll do whatever you feel comfortable with."

"Thank you. Here, I'll let you talk with Brianna."

"Austin?" Brianna asked.

"Yeah."

"Thank you."

"No problem."

"Well, good night."

"Good night, Brianna." I think we both wanted to say more, but neither of us knew what it would be that we'd say. At least I didn't know. What with Robbie never very far out of the picture.

The next weekend the girls had another wedding reception on Saturday night, so on Friday night, Sophie and I and Brianna went bowling. Except Brianna didn't bowl. In fact she didn't even sit with us, but nearby in spectator seating.

Brianna had helped Sophie with makeup and done her hair, so she looked good.

"You look very nice," I told her.

She shrugged. "I don't look like myself."

"It's okay to have a variety of looks. You know, it's like some days wanting spaghetti and other days wanting a hamburger. It's not that one is better than the other. It's just a little variety, that's all."

She thought about it. "Okay."

I bowled first, purposely knocking down only one pin so as not to intimidate her. "Now it's your turn," I said.

"I don't know how to bowl."

"It doesn't matter. This is just for fun. Just enjoy yourself."

She took a deep breath. "Okay."

She rolled two gutter balls and came and sat down next to me. "I didn't even get one."

"You will before the night is over."

She did. On our second game, she bowled a 32. We were both very happy with that score.

After we finished bowling, the three of us went to a pizza place. Because we were on a date, Sophie rode next to me in the truck, with Brianna next to her. Sophie didn't say much, and playing her role as tag-along, Brianna didn't say anything, which meant there were long periods of silence while I tried to think of another question to which Sophie usually gave either a yes or no answer.

At the restaurant, Brianna sat alone at a nearby table while Sophie and I slid into a booth.

After we placed our order, the silence was killing me. I

looked over at Brianna, sitting all alone, and it occurred to me how ridiculous it was, pretending she wasn't there.

"Hey," I whispered to Sophie. "See that girl over there?"

"Which one?" she asked, looking around.

"Don't stare," I hissed. I gestured with my head, "The one sitting alone at that table."

She looked over at Brianna, who was sipping a soda through a straw and acting as though we weren't sitting just a few feet away. "Brianna?"

"Shh. Not so loud. Do you know her?" I asked softly.

Sophie looked confused. "Sure."

I leaned forward across the table toward Sophie, and said quietly, "I've heard about her. People say she's a loner. Has no friends. I guess that's true. Look at her, sitting there, all by herself."

Sophie began to play along. "Should we do something?"

"How about we invite her over to join us?"

"Okay."

I stood up and walked over to where Brianna was sitting. When she looked up at me, I said, "Excuse me, Miss. My friend and I were wondering if you'd like to join us at our booth?" She looked a little confused, but I took her by the hand and brought her back to where Sophie was watching and waiting.

When Brianna slid into the booth next to Sophie, it was the first time I ever saw Sophie smile. Not a big smile. But it was a start.

An hour later we were done eating our pizza and on our way home. The conversation between the three of us had picked up and we'd even shared a laugh or two.

Even so, Sophie asked me, "Will you take me home first?"

"If you want."

"Thank you."

A short time later, in Sophie's apartment parking lot, I opened the passenger-side door, which meant Brianna had to get out first and then Sophie.

"Did you have a good time tonight?" Brianna asked her.

"It was okay, I guess," she said.

"Would you go out with Austin again if he asked you?"

"I guess so."

"Is it okay if Austin walks you to your door?" Brianna asked.

We both could see Sophie panic. "Can you come with us?" she asked Brianna.

"Of course."

We got to her door.

"Would you like Austin to give you a hug?" Brianna asked.

"No," she said quickly.

"Thank you for going out with me, Sophie," I said. "I had a great time."

She wouldn't make eye contact but nodded.

Brianna and I had turned to leave and were walking away, when Sophie called after us.

"Can we do a group hug?" she asked.

"We can totally do that," Brianna said.

We went back to her and did a brief group hug.

"Thank you both," Sophie whispered.

A short time later, Brianna and I were alone as I drove her to her apartment.

"You were amazing tonight," she said.

"I only bowled a 79."

"You know what I mean. It was so good to see Sophie begin to relax around you."

"Yeah, I think she did, a little."

"I can hardly wait to write Robbie and tell him what a hero you were tonight."

"Tell him I'm madly in love with Sophie," I said.

She paused. "Is that true?"

"No."

"Then why would you suggest I tell him that?"

"So he doesn't worry about you and me."

"Should he worry about you and me?"

I could see that I'd dug myself a trap. "No, of course not. You and I are just friends."

She let out a sigh of relief. "Yes, that's it exactly. We're just friends."

"Can I give you a hug at your door?" I asked.

A long pause. "I'm not sure if you should."

"If you're not sure, then I won't do it. I was just talking about a friendly hug."

"You mean like a hug for your future sister-in-law?" she asked.

Ouch! What a mood destroyer. "Yes, exactly."

"Well, maybe it would be all right, if that's all it is."

Actually, we did hug, and it was a long hug, but not like passion-filled, more like we just felt very much at home being in each other's arms.

What I got out of this experience with Sophie was a deep anger at the jerk who had done so much damage to her.

The next night I hauled Brianna and Sophie to a wedding reception just outside of Provo.

At first I wondered how it was that I was able to walk around, sit down next to anyone, and never be noticed. Eventually I came up with some reasons. First of all, I'm not ruggedly handsome. Picture Harry Potter with hair the color of sand, his hairline making the letter M on his forehead, and you pretty much know how I look. I look like somebody who, as a missionary, would be assigned to manage the fleet of mission cars, and after his mission would be called to be a financial clerk in a campus ward, all of which did happen to me. I do my work, I'm efficient, but I don't call attention to myself. No girl in any of my classes, upon first seeing me, would think, *I've got to meet that guy.* Instead she might think, *I need to remember to give my tithing to the bishop on Sunday.*

Another reason why I felt invisible at these wedding receptions is that there are basically only two groups there—friends of the bride and friends of the groom. So no matter what group the person you are sitting next to is in, if he or she doesn't know you, they will assume you're in the other group.

Also, of course, I never sat down and started a conversation. I just sat there, watching and listening to everything that was going on around me.

Right at the beginning of this reception, I watched three cute girls, maybe four or five years old, who started dancing to the music. They looked so happy, so uninhibited, so anxious to celebrate the occasion by dancing. They were smiling, surrendering themselves to the joy they felt from moving their bodies to the music.

But then I noticed the teenage girls. They were not dancing. They seemed frozen in place, like the last thing in the world they would ever do is to go out on the dance floor and dance by themselves.

And then I watched Sophie, how carefully controlled every motion was, how she never looked directly at anyone, especially any guy her age. I knew why. She'd been taken advantage of by an older boy when she was in the eighth grade. I wondered if she had once been like those younger girls I was watching dance to the music—so uninhibited, so eager to celebrate their happiness by dancing.

And suddenly I had things I wanted to say to guys. Things they needed to hear about the damage some of them do to girls.

But how would I do this?

That was the unknown.

On Friday night of the next weekend, the girls played for another wedding reception.

Afterwards, we picked up a bucket of chicken and went out to our favorite parking spot in the mountains and ate it. After we finished, Brianna insisted I play the harmonica for them. They both applauded and cheered me on after each song. And, truthfully, I was getting better, having practiced a little that week.

I asked Sophie if she'd go out with me the next night. She said she would like that very much. "Brianna and I have talked this week," she said. "So I'm okay doing this again." She took a deep breath. "Maybe even without Brianna this time."

"Either way would be great," I said.

Saturday morning I went out and cleaned my pickup. When I originally brought it to school, I didn't think I'd be hauling girls around in it. It had always been a farm vehicle that had been left in a leaky barn during winter, so there were plenty of rust spots on it. The seat had been duct-taped over in places where the fabric had ripped. It badly needed new seat covers and a paint job.

I let my imagination kind of run wild and ended up designing not only new paint and upholstery but also some racing stripes that would make it look like a classic.

That night the three of us went bowling again. In our second game, Sophie picked up a spare. When she turned around to celebrate with us, her eyes were alive and she was happy, and for a minute, she reminded me of those four-year-old girls I'd seen dancing together at the wedding reception—so happy with life and with the pleasure of movement.

It was so good to see, but it only lasted a moment. It ended when she saw some guy in the next lane leering at her. And I don't blame him for that because she is a beautiful girl, especially when she's happy. But the way he was looking at her must have reminded her of an earlier experience, and it killed the moment, and, actually, the rest of the evening.

We only bowled one game and then she asked us to take her home. Outside her place, Sophie asked me to walk her to her door.

Brianna stayed in my pickup while I walked Sophie to her door. She looked at me for a long time and then asked, "Do you want to kiss me?"

"I don't know, Sophie. Why do you ask?"

"That's what guys want, isn't it?"

"I don't know about other guys. I guess sometimes that's true."

"You've been so nice to me. Am I expected to pay you back with a kiss?"

"You don't owe me anything, certainly not that, especially if it would be difficult for you."

"It would be very difficult for me." She sighed. "But I don't want to lose you."

"You mean as a friend?"

"Yes, as a friend."

"I will always be your friend, Sophie, even if we never kiss."

It took her a while to process that, but when she did, she looked at me and with tears in her eyes, said softly, "Thank you. Good night."

"Good night, Sophie."

When I got back in the truck, Brianna asked, "How did it go?"

"Good."

"Did she say she'd had fun?"

"Actually, she asked me if I wanted to kiss her."

"She did?" Brianna sounded as though she couldn't believe it. "What did you do?"

"I asked her why she wanted to know. She said it was because she thought that's what guys expect, and that I'd been so nice to her, and she didn't want to lose me. So I guess she was offering to kiss me just as a payback."

"What did you tell her?"

"I told her I would always be her friend, whether we kissed or not."

"Good answer," she said.

"Whoever that guy was who assaulted her, he messed her up big time. That's so despicable."

"Yes, it is."

I pulled into a parking spot on the street in front of Brianna's apartment and walked her to the door.

We hesitated and then we hugged each other. For a long time, actually.

"Can I ask you a question?" I said. "Lately, I've been thinking about kissing *you*. Does that seem like a possibility to you anytime soon?"

She closed her eyes and lowered her head.

"Are you praying for an answer?" I asked.

She opened her eyes and chuckled. "No."

"Take your time."

"Actually, I've also thought about us kissing," she said.

"You have?"

"Yes, several times."

"You've thought about us kissing several times, you know, like one right after the other? Or have you thought several times about us kissing, like just one time?"

She shook her head and smiled. "The second choice."

"Even that's a surprise to me because I didn't think you'd ever think about it."

"Well, we've been spending a lot of time together," she said.

"Yes, we have. Actually though, I'm physically closer to your harp than I am to you, what with having to roll it into and out of every reception we go to, but that's another story."

"My harp loves you," she said with a bit of a smile.

"I'm sure she does. It is a she harp, right?"

"Yes." She sighed. "Us kissing gets a little complicated with me waiting for your brother to get home from his mission."

"Yes, it does, but look at it this way. Wouldn't you agree that many girls who wait two years before their missionary gets home probably kiss a few guys while he's gone?"

"I would guess that's probably true."

"So, really, if you could just think of me as just some random guy that you would have ended up kissing anyway before Robbie gets back, then maybe it'd be okay."

"Except for the fact that you're his brother."

"You know what? I could totally have that annulled."

She laughed at that, but I knew it wouldn't last, and it didn't.

She let her hand rest on my arm. "Picture this. It's ten years from now. I'm married to Robbie. You're married to someone else. Every time we see each other like at a family reunion, wouldn't we feel a little embarrassed that we'd ever kissed each other?"

She had me and I knew it, but I couldn't admit defeat. "Maybe it would depend on if the only reason we kissed was, you know, just to keep in practice."

She looked confused. "I have no idea what you're talking about."

"Well, you know like when a football team divides into

two squads and has a scrimmage game? Everyone knows it doesn't count."

She started laughing.

"What?"

"Guys are *so* weird!"

Time for a new strategy. "Okay, what about this? What if, after just one kiss from me, you totally forgot about my loser brother? What if, for you, it's like the kiss of the century?"

She smiled and shook her head. "You seem very confident about your kisses."

"Oh, yeah, they're amazing. Want to experience one for yourself?"

"Very tempting, but no thanks."

"You sure? Not even for practice, you know, to keep your lips in shape?"

"I'm sure."

"So, no kissing, right?"

"That's right. I need to wait until Robbie gets home from his mission. That's what I promised him, and it's what I promised myself."

"Okay, I'll honor you in that request," I said. "What I mean is, I'm not going to sneak a kiss in when you're least expecting it."

"Thank you. I would like us to continue to be friends, though. Friendship between us can always remain even if I do end up marrying Robbie."

"Okay, I got it," I said.

"In my religion class, my teacher told us that when Joseph Smith wrote to his wife, he often called her his 'true and faithful friend.' That's what I'd like us to be. True and faithful friends."

"That sounds so noble," I grumbled.

Her eyebrows shot up. "You got a problem with nobility?" she asked with a teasing grin.

"Not at all. But what if I'd rather just make out with you?" I joked.

"That would have no meaning."

I laughed. "Maybe not to you, but it would mean a lot to me!"

She laughed again. "Just be my true and faithful friend, okay?"

Time for me to get serious. "I will. I promise."

"I'm going to write Robbie tonight about how wonderful you've been to Sophie. Why don't you write him, too?"

"Okay."

"Can I see a copy of what you send him?" she asked.

"Sure. That way we can be on the same page."

She nodded. "Austin, we *have* to be on the same page! There's no other alternative if you want to keep seeing me."

"All right, I get it. I'll be your true and faithful friend."

That night I wrote a letter to Robbie.

Robbie,
How's missionary work going?
Good, I hope. Set goals in all you do.
That's what I learned on my mission.
Oh, one thing. I'm seeing Brianna. I'm thinking I'd like to marry her some day. Hopefully before you get home from your mission.

NOW, ELDER, IF THAT'S A PROBLEM FOR YOU, THEN MAYBE YOU'RE NOT WORKING HARD ENOUGH. YOU CAN'T LET MINOR THINGS LIKE THIS TAKE YOU AWAY FROM WHY YOU'RE THERE. STAY FOCUSED! YOU NEED TO SET GOALS TOO, LIKE NUMBER OF BAPTISMS, PROSELYTING HOURS, ETC. LIKE I HAVE FOR BRIANNA AND ME. TO BE MARRIED BEFORE YOU COME HOME.

AUSTIN

There, I'd said what I'd been thinking. The only trouble was if I sent the letter or if I even showed it to Brianna, she'd tell me she couldn't see me anymore. And that would be the end of me spending time with her. So I crumpled that one up and wrote another letter.

ROBBIE,

I'M HELPING BRIANNA AND HER FLUTE-PLAYING FRIEND SOPHIE BY HAULING THEM AND BRIANNA'S HARP AROUND TO THEIR WEDDING GIGS. ALSO, I'VE HAD A FEW DATES WITH SOPHIE. SHE'S A BEAUTIFUL GIRL, AND SO TALENTED, ONE OF THE TEN BEST YOUNG FLUTE PLAYERS IN AMERICA!

WORK HARD AND SET GOALS. I LEARNED TO DO THAT ON MY MISSION, AND IT'S A PART OF MY LIFE NOW IN EVERYTHING I DO. I ALWAYS SET GOALS.

LOVE,
AUSTIN

Even though I could privately hope that Brianna and I would some day get together, I knew that there wasn't much I could do while she was still waiting for Robbie. So the only thing left for me was to be Brianna's "true and faithful friend."

Chapter Four

Not much changed between Brianna and Sophie and me for the rest of fall semester. Almost every weekend they had at least one wedding reception to play for, and almost every week I had a date with Sophie. She had enough confidence in me to not need Brianna with us, but most of the time we had her come along with us anyway.

Although I still hadn't fixed up my pickup, I had at least picked out the paint and designed racing stripes to set it off from any other pickup on campus.

As soon as I got home for Christmas break, I called Nathan Hillman, a friend of mine from high school. His dad owned Hillman Auto Body Shop in Layton.

"You still working for your dad?" I asked.

"Yeah, for just a few more days, and then I'm going on a mission. I leave in two weeks."

"Good for you," I said. "That must mean your dad is doing okay now, right?"

"Yeah, he is. He's doing great. The doctor says his cancer

is in complete remission. He can run his business now, so there's nothing stopping me from going."

"I'm glad you're going."

"Thanks. Me too."

"Hey, the reason I called is I want to get my grandfather's old truck fixed up. It has some rust spots and some dents that need to be pounded out, and it needs a paint job. I was also hoping for some racing stripes."

"Great. Bring it into the shop, and I'll give you an estimate."

The next day, when Nathan gave me the bottom-line estimate for the work that needed to be done, I was shocked. It was going to cost about twice what I'd thought it would.

Nathan noticed my expression. "So, what do you think?" he asked.

"Well, I don't know. It's a lot of money. Maybe I'd better wait until summer."

"I won't be able to do it in the summer."

"I know. Sorry."

He cocked his head and looked at the estimate again. "Maybe I could have you do some work for my dad to help defray the cost."

I scoffed. "Yeah, right. Give me a hammer so I can go randomly pound on somebody's new car. That makes total sense."

"Don't worry. I wouldn't let you within fifty feet of one of our customer's cars. This would be something different."

"What?"

"About a year ago I set up a Web site for our shop. My dad thought it was a total waste of time. But my thinking was that when I need to buy something, I don't look in the

Yellow Pages, I go to my laptop and Google whatever it is that I need. So I figured other people must do the same thing. And I was right. Within a few weeks of setting up the site, we started to get business from people who'd found us on-line. I also started a blog for our Web site. Every couple of weeks I write helpful hints for people who want to keep their cars looking good."

"Sounds good, but I still don't know what you want me to do."

"Keep the Web site updated. That means you'll need to call my dad once a week to find out what specials he's run-ning and then put that on the Web site. Oh, and also, about twice a month, write something for the blog."

"What would I write?"

"Most of the time, tips on keeping their cars looking good, but once in a while, if you want, write about anything you want. What we want to do is keep people coming to our site so that when they're in an accident, they'll come to us for whatever body work they need."

Nathan said he'd knock fifty percent off the bill if I'd agree to keep the Web site and blog going while he was on his mission. I was all for that.

We took the idea to his dad, a bald, soft-spoken man who would have been content to let his work ethic and auto-body skills do the advertising for him. He still seemed surprised that people would let a Web site determine where they took their business.

"That sounds good to me," Nathan's dad said and then returned to his work.

As Nathan walked me to the car, he said, "You'll need to call my dad every week and ask him what his special of the week is. He's not a man who does specials of the week, so you'll have to suggest something. I'll give you a print-out of the specials we've run for the past year. Just repeat those each week while I'm on my mission."

"I can do that."

"If you want to come over tonight, I'll show you what I do to manage the Web site."

"That'd be helpful."

"Since my dad started here, two more body shops have opened up in the area, so things are more competitive." He paused. "So what I'm saying is, this is important to both me on my mission and also to my mom and dad."

"I won't let you down."

"I know you won't."

That night Nathan took me through what I needed to do to manage the Web site. It didn't look like it would take more than about an hour a week.

Just before my folks went to bed, I made arrangements for my dad and me to drive to the body shop in the morning so I could leave my pickup for them to work on.

The next morning I was so excited about my pickup I woke up at six. Since the shop didn't open until eight, and my folks weren't up, I went outside to get the newspaper. On especially cold days, our paperboy stayed in the car while his dad drove. He just lobbed it somewhere on our property. On that day he'd lobbed it over in our neighbor's yard. On my way to get it, suddenly Tornado the Terrorist Dog lunged toward me, barking and baring his fangs. I figured I was a dead man. The only thing that saved me was the shortness of his chain. Just before he reached me, his chain took hold and yanked him backwards onto his back.

"You stupid dog!" I yelled at him. "What'd I ever do to you?"

The next morning when I went outside to get the paper, I walked slowly toward him and sweetly called, "Tornado, are you going to wish me a good morning today?"

Once again he charged me, and, once again, the chain stopped him in his tracks.

The next day, though, he wised up and stopped just before he reached the end of the chain. And then, as I went back inside, he continued to bark for ten minutes, which woke up all the neighbors. It was my gift to the neighborhood.

Nathan spent two full days working on my pickup. When I went in to pick it up, I was blown away by how amazing it looked. I could hardly wait to show Brianna. I thought about driving to her home in Fillmore to show it off and to also see if she'd go out with me on New Year's Eve. But when I phoned her to ask her about it, she told me that would be difficult to explain to Robbie, so I dropped the idea. I stayed home instead and studied up on how to maintain the finish on a new car so I could write something reasonable for Nathan's Web site.

The Sunday after Christmas, I attended Nathan's farewell. At his house later for lunch, I admitted I was having some misgivings about writing about car maintenance twice a month for two years.

"Don't worry," he said. "You'll do okay. Besides, my dad isn't going to ever look at the Web site. All he cares about is if it brings in some business. And I'll never look at it while I'm on my mission, so just relax and enjoy the experience. If you get tired of writing about cars, write about something else."

"Okay, thanks, I'll do that."

When Sophie, Brianna, and I got back to Provo for winter semester, the first thing I did was to take them for a ride in my tricked-out pickup. They loved it.

We also went bowling. During Christmas break, Brianna had created a deck of cards especially made for bowling. Like one card said, "Bowl backwards." Another read, "Bowl left-handed," and another "Bowl like a werewolf." And so on. Before each of us bowled, we had to pick a card. We loved making each other laugh. And now even Sophie joined in.

On the second Saturday in January, Brianna and Sophie played for another wedding reception. While I was wandering around, trying to keep myself from being too bored, I overheard a man and his wife arguing. I wanted to tell him he was being a jerk and that he needed to at least try and understand what his wife was saying instead of arguing with everything she said.

I need to try and talk some sense into guys like him, I thought. *But how?*

And then it hit me. All I had to do was to use a section of my blog to deal with relationships.

Even though I'd written on the blog the day before about the effects of highway salt on car finishes, I decided to add another entry. My first effort grew out of seeing firsthand how much trauma Sophie had gone through because of what some guy had done to her.

Here it is.

Guys,

I know we never talk about it, but the truth is we're messing other guys' lives up. I'll tell you how. If a guy's wife was traumatized because of some abusive act that some idiot did to her long before she met her husband, then both the husband and the wife have to deal with that every day of their lives.

How many women dread intimacy with their husbands because of what some idiot did to her when she was still just a girl? Thousands. So who do we blame? We blame the woman. It's always, "my wife is messed up." But who should we blame? The jerk who did that to her!

So, let's make a deal. I won't mess up your future wife if you won't mess up mine.

What do you think? Let me know. Oh, my name is Steve-O. I don't actually work at Hillman Auto Body in Layton, Utah, but I'm good friends with the owner and his son and can vouch for the good work they do. I work at a body shop in Schenectady, New York. So I'm Steve-O from Schenectady.

To keep any readers from being confused, I set up two icons, the first titled "Auto Body Advice" and the other "Random Thoughts about Life."

There are thousands of blogs. Most of them are only visited by friends and relatives, so I didn't really expect to receive any feedback from what I'd written.

And I didn't for a couple of weeks. And then a woman customer visited the site and read what I'd written. She was so impressed she called into a Salt Lake City radio talk show and recommended my blog. The host looked at it that night and mentioned it again the next day on the air.

The next day I got this response:

> Steve-O,
>
> I just want you to know you're right on target. I was raped by a guy six years older than me when I was not even in my teens. From that point on I would like get physically sick if anyone tried to touch me. I never should have gotten married because I've been no good for my husband. And it's like what you said, he blames me, not the guy who messed me up. If this terrible thing had never happened, both my husband and I would be a whole lot happier now. One thing, I am getting counseling now, and it's actually helping. I am so grateful to my husband for staying with me. Thanks for bringing this up. I hope it helps. Keep up the good work, okay?

Because of what she'd written, I decided to write something once a week for "Random Thoughts about Life."

> January 24
>
> Guys, we often refer to the woman we're dating as a girl or a chick. But I'm just going to call them all women. For two reasons: (1) To me a girl is like twelve years old and I don't want anyone to get confused about who I'm referring to. (2) They're not chicks. They're women. We need to treat them with respect.

Okay, here we go. Guys, what does a woman need from you that's more important to her than anything else? She needs a true and faithful friend. Someone who will do his share of the work around your house or apartment. Someone who will be there for her when she's going through a hard time. That will take time. It might mean you don't always go golfing every Saturday just so you can help her around the house once in a while. Or that sometimes you go with her to a symphony concert instead of watching a football game. It means your sports car hobbies do not trump what she needs from you. Try that for a week and tell me how it goes.

These were the responses:

From Joe:
If you want to spew out this touchy-feely garbage, do it on another Web site. This is an insult to all us hardworking guys who take pride in our vehicles. What is your problem anyway?

From Deborah:
All the secretaries in our office give you a standing ovation! Keep it up, Steve-O! We love you!

From Freddie:
Okay, I did what you said, and I got to say it worked like a charm! My wife and I have never been happier. Okay, so I did my miss my usual

bowling with the guys last Saturday night, but
my wife has more than made up for it. Thanks
for helping me get my act together!

After that, my blog took on a life of its own. At least for
me. I spent every Saturday morning working on the message.
All through the week, I'd read the feedback readers were giving me. The rest of the week I tried to live up to what I was
telling other guys to do. For me it was mostly about trying to
be a true and faithful friend to Brianna.

It mostly worked. Once in a while, though, I'd tell myself I was wasting my time with Brianna when I could be
spending time with someone who wouldn't walk away from
me in June when her missionary came home. Sometimes
I felt I was nothing more to Brianna than just a furniture
mover who transported her harp all over Utah County on
the weekends.

On the last Friday night in January, at a wedding reception, I spent time listening in on what guys said to women
they had just met and were trying to impress. From that experience came this:

January 31

Ten Things You Must Never Say to a Woman

Guys, let's say you're out with a woman for the
first time, and you want to make a good first impression. Here are Ten Things You Should Never
Say to Her:

1. "I've gone on and on telling you about me
for the last hour, and I haven't really heard much
from you. So, what do you think about me?"

If you brag about yourself, then she'll think that's what you always do with every woman you're with. But now you're with her, and she's unique. Find out what is amazing about her by asking her questions about herself.

2. "Do you happen to have a roommate a couple of years younger than yourself?"

When you're with her, you need to focus your attention on her.

3. "You don't mind if I check my emails and text while we're talking, do you?"

Maintain eye contact with her. Don't divert your attention. Don't text while you're with her. Don't check your voice mail. Don't check your emails. It's all about her. Every woman you're with deserves that kind of attention.

4. "Look, if you don't like your job, just quit!"

Don't solve her problems for her. Just be a listening ear. Say things like "Really?" or "Oh, no" or "I can't believe your boss said that."

5. "Look at that waitress! She is so hot!"

Saying something like this makes you sound like you're in junior high. Guys, all women deserve our respect. And while you may think you're giving a compliment to that woman who you say is hot, you are at the same time slamming the woman you're with, and every other woman.

6. "I know a good diet you might want to try. My mom lost forty pounds on it."

Recently at a wedding reception, I overheard some guy actually say this to the woman he was with. Unbelievable, right? That is so insulting! It implies that she will only be acceptable to you when her weight is a certain value, determined by you. It's bad enough the media glorifies women who look like girls. You certainly do not need to be a part of that.

7. "I can't believe you voted for him!"

Arguing about politics seldom brings two people together, especially on the first date.

8. "Exactly why did you break up with the last guy you were going with? Or did he break up with you?"

It's none of your business. Don't ask about her last romance and don't tell her about yours. At least, certainly not on the first date.

9. "How many children do you want?"

If you're going to ask a woman you're seeing this question, wait until you're nearly engaged to her.

10. "Last night I totally made it to Level Ten on *Star Crew Down: The Final Episode!*"

Do you really want her to know you're that much into video games? For most women that would be a deal breaker.

I was surprised at all the responses I got. This one, in particular, stood out.

From Candace:
Steve-O,

All of us gals at work were laughing our heads off reading this. We've heard every one of those dumb things from guys. But what about things women should never say to a guy? We'd all like to know that, too!

To Candace from Steve-O,

Thanks to you and all your friends at work! Okay, here's a list of things women should never say to a man:

1. "You're not thinking of trying to fix that yourself, are you? We need to call someone who actually knows what he's doing."

2. "You have no idea where we are right now, do you?"

3. "How old were you when you first realized you were going bald?"

4. "We need to talk."

5. "You don't exercise at all, do you? I can tell."

6. "Tell me what you're thinking." (Women, believe me, you'll always be disappointed in his answer.)

7. "The guy I was out with last week was such a

good dancer. I wish he were here so he could teach you a few things."

8. "What are you going to do if you can't get another job?"

On the first Tuesday in February, Brianna called me at four-thirty in the morning. She sounded awful. She said she was sick and asked me to come and give her a blessing.

"My roommate knows you're coming so she'll let you in and show you to my room. Please hurry."

If I was going to administer to her, I needed another Melchizedek Priesthood holder. I asked my roommate Darren to get up and help me. We put on our suit pants, white shirts, and ties. Then I drove as fast as I could on the snowy streets to her apartment.

The lights were on, and when we came to the door, her roommate opened it and showed us into Brianna's room.

When we walked in, she struggled to sit up in bed.

"What's wrong?" I asked.

"I don't know. I feel awful. I'm afraid it might be the flu."

"You want me to take you to the hospital?"

"No. Just give me a blessing."

I handed the oil to Darren and asked him to anoint. After he finished, I placed my hands on Brianna's head and gave her a blessing.

At first, I wasn't sure what to say, but words gradually came as I blessed her to get better.

At one point in the blessing, I opened my eyes and looked at my hands on her head. I felt that this was a sacred experience, and I was glad I was living good enough that I could be asked anytime to use my priesthood to give a blessing to someone I cared about. Like Brianna for example.

I asked her roommate if it would be okay for me to stay with her until she felt better. She said it would be okay because she'd been sleeping on the couch most of the night anyway.

"I'm probably not supposed to be here now," I said.

She shrugged. "It's okay. It's almost morning. I'll leave a note for the other girls so they won't freak out if they see you here."

I offered to drive Darren back to our apartment, but he said it wasn't far and he'd just walk.

Brianna's roommate wrote a note about me being there and taped it on the bathroom mirror.

I sat on a chair in Brianna's room, watching her settle into a sound sleep, and soon fell asleep also.

Her roommate came into the room a little after seven, grabbed the clothes she was going to wear for the day, and then left to go change in the bathroom. Just before eight she came in again and told us she was leaving for school.

About half an hour later, Brianna suddenly sat up and threw up all over her bedding. "I'm so sorry," she whispered.

"It's okay. Let's move you onto the couch." I helped her into the living room, got a blanket she hadn't thrown up on, put it around her, and got a glass of water so she could rinse her mouth out into a bowl.

Almost immediately, she fell back to sleep on the couch.

All my life, I'd hated throwing up or being around anyone who threw up. To me, there was nothing worse than the smell and the mess. So I struggled not to let on how I was feeling.

Holding my breath, I pulled the sheets off her bed as well as the blanket she'd gotten messy. I took them downstairs to the laundry room, and trying not to gag, dumped it all into a laundry basin, rinsed it off, and then put it all in a washer. I didn't have any quarters so I used the changer on the wall and got the washer going. I then went back upstairs to see how she was doing. She was still sleeping so I opened her bedroom window to let in a little fresh air but only for a few minutes because it was so cold outside. And then I went back to the basement to wait for her bedding to be done.

A little over an hour later, I returned to her apartment and made her bed. Then I drove to my apartment and shaved, took a shower, and sent e-mails to the teachers of the classes I would be missing that morning. After that I drove to a grocery store and bought some chicken noodle soup, 7-Up, and saltine crackers, which is what my mom always gave me when I was sick to my stomach.

Brianna woke up at eleven-thirty and saw me sitting in a chair next to her.

"You're still here?"

"Yeah, I'm still here."

"Thank you."

"No problem. How do you feel?"

"Better. Thanks for the blessing."

"Some blessing, right? We give you a blessing and you hurl."

"It's just what I needed to do. I feel much better now." She sat up. "I need to go to the bathroom now. I'll be right back."

"Yeah, sure."

When she came back, I could tell she'd brushed her hair. "I feel much better," she said. "I know you have things to do today, so you can go now. Thank you so much for losing sleep and getting up in the middle of the night and staying with me. I can't believe you'd do that for me."

"I'd do it for anyone, Brianna, not just you."

"I know that. That's why I love you." She cleared her throat. "I mean love, in the sense that . . ."

"I might end up as your future brother-in-law?"

She laughed. "Yes, exactly. That kind of love."

We were both feeling a little awkward, so I said, "Oh, if you want to get back in bed, I washed and dried your bedding."

That got to her. "You did? Thank you."

"No problem. Also, if you're feeling better, I got you some chicken noodle soup, some 7-Up, and some saltine crackers."

"Oh, Austin. I'm embarrassed. You didn't need to do all that."

"It was no trouble. I just know that those things taste good after you've been sick."

I don't know how to describe the look she had on her face. She looked sad, but not a bad kind of sad. It was more like . . . like she was trying to figure something out.

"Is something wrong?" I asked.

She smiled and shook her head. "No, nothing's wrong. I just can't believe you'd go to all that trouble for me."

I nodded and before I left I told her to call me if she needed me to run any errands for her.

She didn't call me, so that was good. It meant I could

take care of all the meaningless details of my life instead of being with her.

Our relationship changed after that. I think it was because she knew I would do anything for her when she needed my help.

Which led me to another posting on my blog.

Saturday, February 7

Here's a multiple choice question for all you jalopy jockeys:

What's the best thing you can do to improve your relationship with the special woman in your life?

a. When she's outside shoveling the driveway, walk outside with your shirt off and show her how strong and manly you are. That'll be a big turn-on for her.

b. When she's sick, stay with her and take care of her even if it means you lose sleep or miss work.

c. Women love competition from other women, so tell her how hot the new secretary at work is.

d. Buy her the new video game "Killing Machine Two—The Ultimate Revenge."

This brought a flurry of replies. Here's one.

Steve-O,

I'm still in high school so I'm not sure if you'll want to hear from me, but last October I was in a car accident, and it nearly killed me. My friend Michael from one of my classes has visited me nearly every day, telling me what we did in class, and helping me with the homework, but mostly just talking to me. Before that I didn't really pay much attention to him. He's kind of short and pudgy, but let me tell you something, I care about him more than any other guy I've ever known, I guess because I know he cares about me. He's actually the only real guy friend I've ever had. I'm getting better and will soon be going back to school. And when I do I'm going to be spending my free time with Michael. So it's clear to me that the answer to your quiz is b.

Keep up the good work educating guys, okay? They really need it!

Ashley

A few days later, on one of our threesome dates, Sophie told us that a cello player had asked her out.

"Sophie, that's fantastic! Tell us about him!" Brianna said excitedly.

I wasn't so positive about the whole thing. "What kind of a guy is he?"

"Well, for one thing, I don't freak out when I'm with him," she said. "He's *so* funny! He makes me laugh all the time."

"That's good!" Brianna, Sophie's cheerleader, cried out. "Austin makes me laugh, too. What's this guy's name? Tell us all about him!"

For the next hour Sophie did exactly that. We learned that his name is Christopher, that he'd served a mission in Spain, that he was tall, skinny, and wore glasses that made him look smart, which apparently he actually was. That he was soft-spoken, was actually majoring in mathematics, and hoped some day to teach at a university. Oh, and also that he's from Provo and his dad teaches at BYU. She said Christopher was at BYU on an academic scholarship.

"And so you just believe everything he tells you?" I asked skeptically.

Brianna laughed and elbowed me in the ribs. "No guy is good enough for your little girl, is that right, Dad?"

"All I'm saying is I want to meet him."

A few days later, Sophie invited Brianna and me to eat dinner with her and Christopher at her apartment.

Okay, on the surface, I have to admit Christopher looked perfectly safe for Sophie. But I wasn't going to take any chances. After we'd eaten, I asked if I could talk with him privately.

"I suppose the only reason you play the cello is because it's a good way to meet girls, right? I mean why else would anyone do that?"

He looked at me with a puzzled expression on his face. "I started in third grade."

"So?"

"I wasn't much thinking about meeting girls in third grade. Were you?"

"Well, no, but hey, *I'm* fairly normal."

He turned away but not before I saw the stupid grin on his face.

I hated this guy. "Let me ask you a question, would you take a bullet for Sophie?"

"Actually, all I want to do is to take her to a play on campus. I doubt if there will be much shooting going on."

I realized I was gripping the arms of the chair I was sitting in. And I went on. "Sophie is . . . very special to Brianna and me. We wouldn't want anything to happen to her."

"I know. I feel the same way. We're becoming good friends."

What could I say? "Okay, I guess you can take her out."

"Thanks. Are you going to shadow us the whole time we're together?"

"Why would you think I'd do that?"

"Sophie thinks you will."

"Do I need to do that?" I asked.

"No, you don't."

And so I reluctantly gave him permission to take Sophie to the play as long as he got her home by midnight.

On the Friday night that Sophie was out with Christopher, Brianna invited me over to her apartment to show me how to make a pie.

As usual, her roommates were gone on dates so we had the whole place to ourselves. Not that we needed that. We could have had both sets of parents with us and it wouldn't have changed anything we did.

"You think Sophie's okay?" I asked.

"Yeah, I do."

"You want to go see for sure?"

"No, our little girl has grown up. You've got to let her go."

"I suppose." I sighed. "So now it's just you and me."

Her eyebrows did a quantum leap. "What are you saying?" she asked. "Am I boring you?"

"No, not at all. It's just that when we were with Sophie, we had a reason to be together and now, it's just because we're, well, friends."

"Can I tell you something?" she asked. "I love being with you. And I respect you more than any other guy I've ever met."

"Thank you. Well, Robbie will be home in June. You'll have even more to value about him after his mission. Attributes he didn't even have before his mission."

She picked up a measuring cup and slammed it down on the counter. "Why must you always bring him up when we're together? Don't you think I get sick of hearing about him all the time?" She stormed into her room and slammed the door behind her.

I stood there and waited. But she didn't come out.

After a few minutes, I went to her door and knocked. "The oven dinged. Should I put the pie in now?" I asked through the door.

"Yes."

"The lower or the upper rack?"

"The lower. Put a cookie sheet under it so if anything spills over, it won't mess up the bottom of the oven."

"Okay."

I did what she told me to do and then went back to her door. "How long does it need to cook?"

"Forty-five minutes."

"Okay. I'll set the timer. Are you going to come out again or should I just go home?"

No answer.

I did what she'd told me to do and returned to the door to her room.

"Okay, the pie's in. I set the timer, too. I guess I'll just go home now, okay?"

She opened the door. I could tell she'd been crying. "Please, just hold me."

"Okay, sure."

I held her for like five minutes. "Could we sit down?" I finally asked.

She nodded. We sat down on the couch, and I continued to hold her. She wasn't crying though, so that was good.

I held her until the timer went off. That's right. Forty-five minutes later.

"Austin, please kiss me," she whispered.

"Actually, you know what? The timer just dinged," I stammered.

"I don't care. Just kiss me."

I kissed her lightly on the lips.

She pulled away. "Not like that." She threw her arms around me and kissed me like she meant it. Like we were in love with each other.

This went on for a couple of minutes and then I pulled away to catch my breath. I must have sounded a little panicky. "Okay, let me tell you something, okay? I'm really worried . . . you know . . . about the pie. We don't want it to get burned, right?"

She pushed me away, jumped up, stormed into the kitchen, and took the pie out of the oven.

When she came back, she was mad. "Go home, Austin! I don't want you here anymore!"

"But I haven't had any of the pie."

"That's all you care about, isn't it? It's never about me! It's always about Sophie or Robbie or some stupid pie, right?"

It was then I realized I was dealing with Psycho Girl.

"All I am to you is Robbie's girl, right? You don't care anything about me, do you? You'll be so relieved when he comes home, won't you, so you can be totally done with me. I'm right, aren't I?"

"No, that's not true. I love you."

"Like you love Sophie?"

I had by this time given up. "What do you want me to say?"

"I want you to tell me the truth! Do you love me enough to write Robbie and tell him to forget about me because you're going to ask me to marry you?"

"Now? Why would I do that? My gosh, Brianna, it's only like four months until he gets home. Can't you wait another four months?"

"No! I'm sick of waiting for someone I can't even remember! I'm starting to think of him the same way I used to think of Santa Claus. I know I'm supposed to love him but I can't remember why, except he leaves me presents under the tree!"

"Robbie leaves you presents under the tree?"

She grabbed my shoulders. "Let me make this perfectly clear! I'm sick of pretending that I still care about him when it's you I love."

"Me? When did this happen?"

She lowered her head and let out a big sigh. "I don't know. But it's happened."

"What do you want me to do?" I asked.

"Well, for starters you could tell me you love me. And would it kill you to at least one time talk about us getting married?"

"Wait a minute! What about that talk you once gave me about how awkward it would be at family reunions if we got married?"

"So we won't go to any family reunions! It's no big deal."

"We'll talk about this again, maybe on Sunday after church. We'll both be more, well, spiritual . . . and calm . . . then."

That pretty much sent her over the edge. She grabbed the pie, ran to the door, opened it and held the pie out, as if she were about to toss it away.

"If you want any of this pie, tell me you love me. You've got ten seconds. Ten . . . nine . . . eight . . . seven . . . six . . . five . . ."

"Wait!"

She stopped counting. "Yes?"

"You're not treating me like a friend if you demand things of me that I'm not willing to do."

"Go home then, Austin! I can't be with you anymore now that I know how you really feel about me." She threw the pie as hard as she could. It landed on the snow about twenty feet from where she'd tossed it.

Outside, on my way back to my apartment, I thought I'd just check on the pie. It had landed on top of a big pile of snow. It had broken into two large pieces plus several smaller pieces when it landed.

I had just picked up the largest piece when she looked

out the window, saw me, and came outside. "I should have known you'd do that! Have you no respect at all for me?"

"It's just a pie, for crying out loud!" I complained.

"Austin, listen to me! Put that pie down right now! Leave it on the ground and go back to your apartment."

"No! It's my pie, too! I helped make it!" To spite her, and while she was watching, I used both hands to cram the largest pie fragment into my mouth, then reached down with both hands, scooped up the other large piece, including some snow that came with it, and stuffed it all into my mouth. I then yelled something at her, which luckily she couldn't understand because of all the food in my mouth. I then trudged to my pickup and drove off.

The next day was Valentine's Day. After what had happened the night before, I was at a loss to know what to give Brianna. I ended up going to a florist shop and buying a single rose in its vase. I chose the kind of Valentine's card that if you were in third grade, you could have given it to your teacher. I scribbled this on the card, "Thank you for being the best friend I've ever had. Austin."

I was actually grateful she wasn't home when I dropped her Valentine gift at her apartment.

"Who are you?" one of her roommates asked.

"I'm the brother of the guy she's waiting for on his mission."

"Oh, yeah. You're the guy who helped when she got sick, right?"

"Yeah, that's me. We've become good friends."

That afternoon I wrote the following in my blog:

Saturday, February 14

What do you do when the woman in your life is completely irrational? When she says things that don't make any sense? When you can't even begin to understand what she's saying?

I'm not going to answer that question because the truth is I don't have a clue what the answer is. Can anyone out there help me out?

I got some good responses.

From Derek:

Been there, done that, Buddy!

With my wife it happens every once in a while. What I do when it happens is go fishing or hunting. If you ask me, that's why so many guys are into outdoor sports.

From Audrey:

Guys, look, it's okay to go fishing or hunting, just remember to come back. You two need a break from each other once in a while. Chances are she won't be like this for very long. When you come back though, bring lots of chocolate!

From Charlene:

I don't buy Audrey's take on this, that all women become basically insane once in a while. If your woman is mad at you, then I'm thinking it was something you did, so you'd better start

thinking about what it might be and then go ask
her to forgive you.

On Sunday after church, Brianna called. She thanked me for the rose and Valentine card and then asked if we could talk. I told her I'd be right over.

It was too cold to take a walk and we didn't want to talk with her roommates around so we went on campus and found a place in the Wilkinson Center where we could sit and talk.

"First of all, I want to apologize for the way I acted Friday night," she said. "I don't know what happened to trigger that."

"It was probably something I said." I figured that was safe to say, since women usually blame everything on men anyway.

"No, it wasn't." She wiped her brow. "I think where I possibly might have gone just a tiny bit over the top was when I demanded you kiss me. And also when I used the M-word. M for marriage."

"Yeah, well, that was a little scary."

"By the way, thank you for not taking advantage of the situation when I was in that state of mind." She paused. "You know, like actually proposing to me for example. I'm very embarrassed about what happened."

"I didn't know what to do," I admitted.

"You did the right thing."

"Sorry about eating the whole pie. But, you know, it was in good, clean snow, and I didn't think it would be a bad thing to do."

That made her laugh. "You're right," she said. "A pie thrown outdoors is open for the taking by any animal that comes across it." She paused. "Not suggesting of course, that you're an animal."

"Well, actually I am, I guess, if you go by the strict definition of animal."

She paused, took a deep breath, and then began again. "Okay, that was Part One of what I needed to say. Let's take a walk for Part Two."

We took another little walk and ended up sitting on a sofa in the N. Eldon Tanner Building on campus. We watched as a student ward left their sacrament meeting and went to Sunday School.

She wouldn't look at me. "I suppose that, from my outburst Friday night, you probably have surmised that I have actually developed . . . shall we say . . . feelings about you that some might possibly interpret as love and affection."

"Yes, I did gather that from what you said to me."

"The easiest thing for me to say to you today is that I must have had a small insanity episode and that I didn't mean a word of it."

"I could certainly understand if you said that," I said.

"But, the truth is, I actually do care about you, and I think it's strong enough to be labeled, for lack of a better word, as, well, love."

"So you're saying you love me?" I asked.

"I wouldn't go that far, but, yes, I would say that it is something very much akin to, well, love."

"I see," I said, still confused

"And how do you feel about me?" she asked.

I knew what I wanted to say, but I knew it would be wrong to say it. "I think right now it doesn't matter how I feel about you. Robbie will be back in four months. I think we should postpone this discussion until you've had some time to be with him."

"That, of course, is what I'd expect you to say. You are such a noble person." She sighed and added a little sarcastically, " . . . as we all know . . . and occasionally regret."

I said, "What if we got engaged and Robbie came back and then you decided he was the one you really wanted? That could be very awkward. And very confusing to our parents."

"Indeed it would be." She paused. "So you're suggesting to me that we continue as before? I mean, that is to say, before the unfortunate pie incident."

"That's what I would suggest."

"That seems reasonable to me." She shrugged. "If that's what you think is best."

I sighed. "I don't see any other alternative. If you and I were to act . . ." I paused while I searched for just the right word. " . . . precipitously, shall we say, I know that my mom and dad would be confused and perhaps even disappointed in me."

She couldn't help but smile. "I have never been in a conversation with a guy where he used the word *precipitously* and also the phrase '*shall we say.*'"

"We're both in new territory. May I just say that I think you are the most beautiful girl I've ever known."

"Is that supposed to clear things up for me?" she asked.

"No, not really. It's just that I never say it to you, but I think about it every time we're together. You have such amazing lips. And, my gosh, your hair! I have a fantasy of having your hair completely cover my face so I can hardly breathe."

She shook her head. "You definitely need counseling," she said with a silly grin.

"Yeah, whatever. Never ask a guy what he's thinking, okay? You'll always be disappointed."

She shrugged. "Apparently neither my lips nor my hair were enough to win you over Friday night."

"Friday night I felt like I was dealing with someone I didn't even know."

"I am truly sorry about that." She turned to me. "Can you at least tell me that you love me?"

I thought about it. "Actually, I don't really think I should do that. We need to wait for Robbie to come back. All your options are open until then. I don't want to take advantage of the current situation. Whatever happens I want to always be your true and faithful friend."

"Like Joseph and Emma?"

"Yes."

"Fair enough."

I touched her hand. "You and I have been together almost every day since I got here in the fall. It's not fair for you to make a decision about Robbie when you haven't seen him for almost two years."

"Remind me again what's good about Robbie?"

I didn't actually want to do this, but for both their sakes, decided I should at least give it a try. "Well, for one thing, he's taller than me. He's got a lower voice than I do. He's a better athlete than I am. He's really a good fisherman, too. Oh, and he's got a good build."

"You're right! I'd totally forgotten about that! Have you ever seen him with his shirt off?" she asked, now full of enthusiasm.

"He's my brother. Of course I have. When did *you* see him without his shirt on?"

"Swimming."

"Oh, okay. So we're okay with waiting for Robbie and his good build to come back from his mission?" I asked.

"Yes, of course. That seems like a prudent course of action to me also."

As we left the building, I reached for her hand.

She pulled her hand away. "What are you doing? After all our talking today, you want to hold my hand?"

"Is that okay?"

"I don't know. I just find it inconsistent, that's all."

"You practically threw yourself at me Friday night, so me wanting to hold your hand seems, by comparison, a relatively harmless thing."

She shrugged. "I will never understand guys."

"Guys are easy. Girls are the ones who are impossible to understand," I said.

"You should go to this blog a friend told me about," she said. "It's on some auto body Web site."

I panicked. "What can a blog on an auto body Web site teach me about girls?"

"That's what's crazy. It's all about relationships."

"Actually, I think I have heard about that blog. I heard it's basically soft porn. If I were you, I'd stay away from it," I lied.

"The guy who told me about it didn't mention anything about porn."

"I think that tells us a great deal about your friend then, doesn't it?"

"You're right. I'll stay away from it. And him."

"Good."

That was a close call. The last thing in the world I needed was for her to be reading my blog.

This is what I wrote the Saturday after our discussion about being true and faithful friends.

Saturday, February 21

How to Be a True and Faithful Friend (to a Woman)

1. Never speak badly of her to anyone. If someone is critical of her, stand up for her.

2. When she needs someone to talk to, take time to listen. Do your best to show empathy.

3. Be true to the friendship you share even when you're mad at her, or when you feel that you've been shortchanged in some way or other, or even when you want to get even. When you're both tired, take care of her needs first instead of your own.

4. Act in such a way that she always feels safe in your presence.

5. When she's been hurt by something you've done, instead of defending your good intentions, start your apology by saying, "I'm sorry I . . ."

6. When she wants to talk, turn off the TV, log out of your laptop, quit playing video games, move what you were reading far away, don't look at your watch. Give her your complete

attention. Look at her when she's speaking. Nod or go "okay" so she'll know you're listening.

7. Understand that she's not perfect but neither are you. Do your best to understand her point of view. Also, cherish her the way she is now.

8. Know when her birthday is and plan ahead of time what you're going to give her. Also know the names of her brothers and sisters. Know what her favorite color is, her favorite dessert, her favorite movie. Learn as much as you can about her by asking her questions.

9. Send her flowers or a card once in a while— not for a special occasion but just to let her know that you're thinking of her.

10. If she loves concerts, go with her. If she likes to go to church, go with her. If she loves to go wind surfing, go with her. Let her teach you what she loves to do and, in turn, you teach her what you love.

Chapter Five

The next time Brianna and Sophie and I were on our way for them to play at a wedding reception, all Sophie could talk about was how amazing Christopher was.

Brianna was supportive and positive, but, for some reason, I was grumpy that Sophie was so happy and excited.

"He asked me to go to devotional with him this week," Sophie said.

"The old 'let's go to devotional together' ploy, huh?" I said cynically.

Brianna turned to me and scowled. "What's that supposed to mean?"

"C'mon, don't you know? That's the best way for a guy who's totally inactive in the Church to give the impression he's like very spiritual."

"Christopher is the elders quorum president in his ward," Sophie said.

I realized that definitely weakened my case, but I wasn't

going to just give up. "See there? He's even fooled the bishop."

"Don't listen to Austin," Brianna said. "He's just being like an over-protective brother."

"I am not over-protective," I said. "What I am is concerned."

"No, what you are is irrational," Brianna joked, and Sophie laughed.

The wedding reception that Brianna and Sophie were playing for was scheduled from 6 to 8 pm. At seven forty-five, Christopher showed up, intending to give Sophie a ride back to her apartment.

He and I sat together, and I began the interrogation. "What exactly are your intentions with regard to Sophie?"

He seemed confused. "I'm not sure what you're asking."

"Are you just out for a good time?"

"Is that bad?" he asked.

"It could be. I guess it depends on your definition of what a 'good time' is."

"I'm confused. Are you Sophie's brother?"

"No, but I am someone who thinks a great deal of Sophie. I don't want her to get hurt."

"Getting hurt is one of the risks of seeing another person, isn't it? I mean if it doesn't work out, one or the other could end up being hurt."

I glared at him. "Let me guess. You've had a philosophy class, haven't you?"

"No, psychology. You're going to be angry and hurt if Brianna and your brother get married, aren't you?"

"Hey, we're not talking about me."

"If you're wondering if I'm going to physically hurt

Sophie, like she was hurt when she was younger, the answer to that question is no. I like her very much, and I think she likes me. She and I have a great deal in common, such as music and love of the arts."

He had me there. I sighed. "I'm sorry. I was way out of line. Sometimes I act like an idiot."

"She's told me what a good influence you've had on her. She's grateful, and, now, I'm grateful."

"Thanks. I apologize for doubting your integrity. I can see she's in good hands when she's with you." I stood up to leave. "Oh, one thing. Yes, I am going to be devastated if my brother marries Brianna."

I went out into the hall and got a drink of water and sat alone, away from anyone, and waited for Brianna to be done so I could haul her harp out to my pickup, and then take her back to her apartment

On our way back to her apartment, Brianna and I talked for an hour about Sophie and Christopher. For both of us, I think, this was like seeing your oldest daughter being courted. Brianna tried to help me feel good about what was happening to Sophie. "It's what we've always wanted for her, isn't it?" she asked.

"Yeah, I guess so. It's just that in a short time I may lose both you and her."

"I will always care about you, no matter what happens."

I let out a long, troubled sigh. "I'll be your favorite brother-in-law, right?"

"Maybe so."

After I dropped her off, I went back to my apartment and wrote my blog for the week.

March 7

My dad was the one who taught me to care about other people. When I was growing up, there was a widow living next door. She had some health problems. My dad and I shoveled her driveway every time it snowed. And in the spring we helped her with her garden. At least once a month we visited her and asked what we could do to help her.

As time went on, my dad got busy at work so he asked me to take the responsibility of looking after her. At first I resented having to shovel her driveway or spend hours weeding her garden. Once, when I complained, he just shrugged his shoulders and said, "That's what it means to be a good neighbor."

It was not until I was nineteen that I finally understood what my dad was trying to teach me, which was that being a good neighbor is what we were put on earth to do. I see that kind of selfless service all around me in my neighborhood, and it gives me great comfort to know that no matter what is thrown at us, as a community we will be able to get through it, mainly because we'll help each other along the way.

Guys, this isn't about doing something just so you can show a girl what a great guy you are. First, become a great guy, care about others, look for opportunities to serve your neighbor, and then, after that, whatever else you want is more likely to come your way.

Thanks, Dad. I finally get it.

Within hours, I had some responses.

From Gertrude:

Steve-O,

How come I've never met a man like you before? My search for a suitable guy so far has been like going to garage sales hoping to find a small nugget of gold but finding nothing but junk. I'd love to find a man who cares about other people and tries to be a good neighbor. Can you tell me where a man like you can be found?

From Steve-O to Gertrude:

They can be found in churches and synagogues. But not all men in those places are pure gold either, so be careful. Watch how he treats his mom and sisters and you'll get a clue how he'll treat you.

From Melissa:

Steve-O, for the past ten years, since I was fourteen, I've been involved with guys who only wanted one-night stands. They're all gone now. So now what do I do?

From Steve-O to Melissa:

> You can start a new life! If you need help do-
> ing it, and if you don't mind being religious, visit
> with a priest or minister and ask him to help you.
> He'll be grateful for the opportunity. The mes-
> sage of most religions is that we can change
> and become closer to God. You can do it! You'll
> be a lot happier if you do.

Near the middle of March, Brianna talked me and Sophie into being in her campus ward's talent show. This is how it went: Wearing formals, Brianna and Sophie walked on stage. I rolled Brianna's harp out from off-stage. I was wearing boots, jeans with a hole in the knee, a wrinkled flannel shirt, and a beat-up cowboy hat.

While I extracted her harp from its dolly, Brianna announced, "Tonight we would like to play a lovely piece for you." She said it with a kind of snooty accent you might expect from someone who thinks she is superior to the rest of the world.

"Doggies! I'd like to play that, too!" I said with a hillbilly accent.

"I'm sorry. This is just for a flute and a harp."

"I play the harmonica."

"I see. Do you happen to know the music to Consolation Number Three by Liszt?" Brianna asked me. She looked at me as though I were nothing more than a hick.

"No, but how good can it be if it only got a consolation prize? I got a consolation prize once in a dog show, and my dog was . . . well . . . a real dog."

"If you could please leave the stage so we can perform our Liszt."

I reached for my shirt pocket. "You want to perform a list? Here, you can perform my list." I looked at the piece of paper. "Okay, first thing I had to do today is plunge the toilet. See, in my apartment, the toilet is always getting clogged. Well, you can imagine how much trouble that is."

"I was actually referring to the composer, Liszt."

"Hey, you're not so great. I can come up with a list of composers too. Like, for instance, well, don't tell me, he's that famous composer who came back."

"I have no idea what you're talking about."

"Wait, I remember now. It's Bach. Get it? He came back and that reminds me of Bach. I use memory tricks to remember things. That's why I'm so smart."

"What memory trick would remind you to get off the stage?"

"C'mon, Girl, just give this a try. One . . . two . . . three . . ."

I began playing "When the Saints Come Marching In." After some shrugging of shoulders between Brianna and Sophie, they joined me on their instruments.

It was great! We got a standing ovation.

After we got off stage and into the hall, Brianna gave me a big hug. "That was so much fun!"

"We're a good team, aren't we?"

"The best!" she said.

I think Sophie might have also hugged me, but Christopher was in the hall with us, so she hugged him instead. But that's okay. Sophie, Brianna, and me, we're all just good friends. Until they both go off and get married to Christopher and Robbie and leave me with only some stupid harmonica.

Brianna invited me to her parents' house in Fillmore, Utah, to watch April Conference. We drove to her place Friday because she wanted to see her younger brother Todd play soccer Friday afternoon. He played for his high school team.

The game didn't get started until a little after six. By that time the wind was blowing hard. Because of the wind and rain most people just parked around the boundaries of the field and watched from their cars.

About forty minutes later the rain turned to snow. The coaches decided to go ahead and just continue playing.

So there we were, Brianna and me, in my pickup with the engine running, the wind blowing up a blizzard, and us barely able to see the game.

At first I just had my arm around her, and then, some-how, I got distracted from the game, and I kissed her. At first she just relaxed in my arms, but then on our second or third kiss, just after spectators started sounding their car horns, she pulled away, suddenly very angry with me. "What just happened?"

"I think one of the teams scored a goal."

She shoved me away. "I'm not talking about the game! We need to talk."

"Why do we always need to talk?" I grumbled.

"This isn't the path we decided to go on. Please stop kiss-ing me."

"Just one more, okay?" I begged.

"No! Listen to yourself! You're totally out of control."

"I am not. The way I see it, if I can still talk, I'm not out of control."

"I'm so disappointed in you, Austin! You know this isn't what we agreed to! I'm going to watch the rest of the game with my mom and dad in the car."

"Let me go with you."

"No!"

"If I don't go with you, they'll suspect something happened between us."

"I don't care what they think. My gosh, Austin, this is hard enough as it is without you adding wood to the fire. Why don't you live up to what we agreed to?"

She got out of the truck and slammed the door.

I wasn't sure if I was still invited to spend the weekend with her and her family or if she wanted me out of her life. I thought maybe I should just go back to Provo and see if Sophie or Christopher could hook me up with some random oboe player or whatever.

After the game was over, Brianna came back to my pickup and got in. It was snowing hard now.

"I thought we'd agreed how things were going to be until Robbie gets back!" she complained, shaking the snow from her hair and coat, but not even looking at me.

"We did agree," I conceded.

"And was kissing me part of that agreement?" She turned to glare at me.

"No."

"So why did you kiss me?"

I had no answer. "I don't know."

"Give me some possible reasons."

I stammered. "Well, you know, I've always been a big sports fan."

She looked at me as though I were crazy. "What has that got to do with us kissing?"

"Well, uh," I said, "watching sports has always been a happy time for me. You know, you watch a football game with friends. You eat nachos and hot dogs."

"And you make out?"

"Well, not always. I would say that pretty much depends on how close the game is. If it's a real close game, you don't usually make out."

"Are you serious? How many times have you made out watching a game?"

"I've never actually done it, okay? I've just thought about it . . . a lot actually."

"With who?"

"Are you asking me who I thought about making out with but never did? That could be a very large number."

"Who did you want to make out with when you were watching a game?"

"In high school that would have been a girl named Brooke."

"Who was she?"

"She was the sister of my best friend. She always watched the games with us."

"How much younger than you was she?"

"Well, actually, she was a year older."

"She was a year *older?*"

"Didn't I just say that? She liked me, too. She always sat next to me, and she let me have some of the nachos from her plate. You never let me do that. With you it's always, 'Get your own plate, Austin. It's more sanitary that way.'"

"What else did she do?"

"She rubbed my back while we were watching the game. You never do that, either. In fact, except for her, nobody else has ever done that."

She shook her head. "Sometimes I feel like I don't even know you," she grumbled.

"Well, I guess that's fair. Sometimes I wonder if I'll end up regretting I ever knew you."

Okay, that was over the top. She started crying.

"I'm sorry I said that. I didn't really mean that."

"Yes, you did mean it," she complained.

I sighed. "Yeah, well, maybe a little."

"Don't worry. This will all be over soon. Robbie comes home in two months."

"That'll be so great for both of us to see him again, right?" I asked.

"Yes, of course," she said with little enthusiasm.

"When he comes home, do you want me to tell him I kissed you a few times, or do you want to tell him that?" I asked.

"I think you should tell him."

"Okay, no problem. I think I'll tell him at the airport while he's still a missionary and has to live mission rules, you know, like the one about not killing people."

"Well, I'm not sure it would be a good idea to tell him with your whole family looking on."

"How about a poster that I could flash him when he first enters the baggage area. Like it could say, 'Welcome home,

Elder Winchester! Oh, I made out with Brianna a couple of times, but you need to get over it.'"

"Very subtle," she said, trying to stifle a smile.

"That's me." I sighed. "The way I look at all this is that we meant well."

"We did. We tried very hard to be noble," she said.

"And, really, we've only had like what? Two kissing, uh, episodes since the beginning of fall semester. So, in a way, it's really a triumph of the human spirit."

She actually smiled. "Well, I wouldn't go that far, but I guess we did okay, considering the feelings we have for each other."

I sighed. "Yeah, it was tough sometimes, though, right?"

"Yeah, it was. Please drive me home. I don't want my folks to be wondering what happened to us."

"Okay. Am I still invited to stay with you guys this weekend?"

"Yes, of course." She paused. "My weakness seems to be wanting to kiss any guy I bake a pie with, while you have a fantasy about making out while watching a football game. I guess it will all balance out as long as one of us stays strong."

"We must promise ourselves, though, never to bake a pie together while watching a football game," I said.

She started laughing. "Yes, that would be the end of us, all right."

"So we're okay?" I asked.

"Yeah, I think we are."

On the way to her house, she sat close to me.

"Oh, there's something I haven't told you yet," she said.

"What?"

"My birthday is Sunday. But I don't want you to get me anything for it, okay?"

"Why not?"

"If you got me something really nice, then once Robbie gets home, if he asks me where I got it, then I'd have to tell him you bought it for me for my birthday."

"What if it's cheap and of no value?"

"Then my folks will wonder what kind of a guy you are. And that would also reflect badly on Robbie."

"So you really want me to get you nothing?" I asked.

"Yes, please, that's what I want."

"Sure, you can count on it."

We watched conference all day Saturday and then I went with her dad and youngest brother to priesthood.

When we got home from priesthood, Brianna's next older sister Monica was there with her husband and baby. I actually got along great with Monica.

About ten o'clock that night, Monica took me aside. "I just wanted to make sure you know that tomorrow is Brianna's birthday."

"Yeah, I know."

"What are you giving her?"

"She asked me not to get her anything."

"Yeah, so what did you get her?" Monica asked.

"Uh, nothing."

"You can't be serious," she said.

"I'm doing what she said for me to do."

"She didn't mean don't get her anything. She meant don't get her anything expensive. You've got to get her something. You'd better go now. There's a gas station about a mile from here. Take a left once you get to the main road."

At the gas station/convenience store, I wandered through the place trying to find something she'd like. Finally I got her an air freshener in the shape of a fir tree, a Big Slurpy, a packet of beef jerky, and a *Keep on Truckin'* baseball hat.

I wanted to keep the Big Slurpy frozen until the next day so I hid it in the freezer in Brianna's folks' kitchen.

That night I used my laptop to write another blog.

April 4

What do you do when your significant other tells you not to buy her a gift for her birthday or your anniversary?

Take it from me. Totally ignore her request. If you don't give her anything, you'll be in deep trouble.

Question: What other things that women say to their men need to be totally ignored?

These were the responses that came into my blog over the next week.

From Bart:

When she tells you that you need to spend more time with the kids. The problem is that she doesn't mean that. What she means is that she needs a break from the kids. When my wife told me I needed to spend more time with the kids, I started taking my older kids fishing with me every Saturday. We'd come back and she'd still be mad at me because we had fun and she had to take care of our baby. It took me a year to figure it out. Keep up the good work, Steve-O! I'm sure you're helping a lot of clueless guys out there, like I used to be!

From Adam:

When she goes, "The steps are so icy." And you go, "Yeah, they are, I nearly fell coming in the house." And then she gets mad at you for saying that.

What she means is, "I need you to get the ice off the steps." Except she'll never say it. I swear woman-speak is like learning a foreign language.

On Sunday morning Brianna and I snacked our way through conference, and then Brianna's mom had a special lunch/birthday party for Brianna.

Her mom and dad gave her a beautiful necklace. Her sister Monica gave her some earrings that matched the necklace. Her brother Todd gave her a BYU hoodie. And then they all looked at me.

"Well, I didn't have time to wrap this, but I guess that's okay, right, because you'd just rip the wrapping off anyway. Okay, my first gift is something I know you'll like because you're always thirsty. Just a minute and I'll go get it."

I went to the kitchen and opened the freezer expecting to see the Big Slurpy I'd bought for her the previous night. But it was gone.

I returned to the living room. "Did someone take the Big Slurpy that was in the freezer?"

"Yeah, I drank it last night," Todd said. "Why? Was that yours?"

"Yeah, it was. It was going to be part of Brianna's birthday present."

He broke out laughing. "You were going to give her a Big Slurpy as a birthday present?"

"That was just one of my many presents to her." I opened the bag. "Plus, there's this and this . . . and this." I handed Brianna the *Keep on Truckin'* baseball hat, the packet of beef jerky, and, to top it off, the air freshener shaped like a fir tree but designed to smell like a gas station restroom. "There you go. Happy Birthday!"

Brianna was in shock.

"Hey, Brianna, if you don't want the jerky, can I have it?" Todd asked Brianna.

Brianna sadly shook her head.

Todd picked up the *Keep on Truckin'* hat, put it on, and then handed it back to Brianna.

"Actually, I don't even want that," Todd said.

Brianna got all emotional on us and ran to her room.

I felt I needed to make an explanation to her family. "Brianna told me she didn't want me to get her a present, so I didn't, but then Monica said I really needed to get her a present, but it was so late by then the only place I could shop was that gas station just up the road."

"It's a very nice hat," Brianna's dad said.

"Yeah, if you're a long-haul trucker!" Todd said, then started laughing again.

"Todd, that will be enough," his mom said.

Stifling a grin, Todd looked at me. "You are in *so* much trouble."

Brianna watched the afternoon session of conference in her room. I wanted to go in there and talk to her but figured it would be a little awkward to just barge into her room without permission, and I was afraid if I knocked, she'd tell me she didn't want to talk to me and Todd would hear it and start teasing me again.

As soon as the closing prayer for Conference was said, I stood up and said, "Well, I really need to be going now. I've got a lot of work to do to get ready for my classes tomorrow." I paused. "Uh, could you ask Brianna if she wants a ride back to Provo? If she doesn't, I certainly understand."

"If she did ride back with you, she could wear her new hat, and you two could give a big shout-out to all the truckers you pass," Todd said, pumping his arm as though he were honking a truck horn.

"I'll go ask her if she wants a ride," her mom said.

It took forever, but finally Brianna's mom came back to the living room. "Brianna says she would like a ride. She'll be just a minute more."

"Are you going to go buy her another Big Slurpy for the trip?" Todd teased.

"Todd, that will be enough," her mom warned.

Wanting to smack him, I said, "I'll be in my pickup waiting. Thank you for your hospitality this weekend."

Todd took one last shot at me. "I hope you'll come back for October conference. Maybe then you could give her a new snow shovel! That'd be almost as lame as what you got her for her birthday!" And then he burst out laughing.

I nodded and walked out to my pickup and waited.

This is it, I thought. *She'll break up with me on the way back. That will free her up for Robbie's return. She was probably looking for an excuse anyway.*

Five minutes later she came out and got in my truck. She had her *Keep on Truckin'* hat in her hand. Not on her head of course.

"Sorry to keep you waiting," she said politely.

"No problem."

We drove for maybe fifteen minutes without either of us saying a thing.

And then suddenly I heard a small eruption of sound from Brianna. I looked over at her, thinking she might be choking.

There was just the hint of a smile on her face.

"A Big Slurpy?" she asked, and then she started laughing. This was like a belly laugh that wouldn't stop. After a moment, I started laughing, too. I pulled over and stopped and put my hazard lights on.

We laughed until our sides ached. And then she removed her seatbelt and made a lunge at me and threw her arms around me and we laughed together.

She insisted on changing places with me so she was in the driver's seat. She put on her *Keep on Truckin'* hat. When a truck passed us, she pumped her right hand a couple of times like she was a trucker operating an air horn. "Keep on Truckin'!" she shouted.

I was gasping for breath, "Please, stop, I can't take any more!"

We traded places and I drove for about half an hour and then I pulled off the road at a rest stop.

"Why are you stopping?" she asked.

"I just wanted to say thanks."

"For what?"

"For not telling me what a jerk I was not getting you anything for your birthday."

"What are you talking about? Truth is you got me four gifts. Oh, that reminds me, do you want to share some of my jerky?"

"Sure, why not?"

I'm sure her intention was, after she ripped off the wrapping, to break it in two equal pieces. But that's not as easy as it sounds.

"Have you got a knife?" she asked.

"No. I've got a pair of pliers and a screwdriver."

"And who knows where they've been, right?"

"They're sterile."

She gave up trying to break it in two. She moved the jerky closer to me. "You start on this end, and I'll start on the other," she said. "When we get near the middle, we'll decide then how many of our germs we want to share."

"You are such a guy!" I said with sincere admiration.

"Thanks," she said. "It comes from having Todd as my brother."

"Oh, yes, Todd, my buddy."

We gave up on the jerky.

"Sorry he gave you such a hard time."

"I deserved it. Let's face it, I'm an idiot."

"No, you're not. You're my best friend, and I will always be grateful for everything you've done for me."

"I feel the same way about you."

"This sounds like we're saying good-bye, doesn't it?" she asked.

"Kind of."

"I'm not sure I'll ever want to do that," she said.

"I won't for sure."

"I can't believe that I would ever pick Robbie over you."

"You might though."

"I told him I'd wait for him. That's all I told him. Just hold on a little longer, Austin. Be the man I believe you are."

"What kind of a man is that?" I asked.

She quoted from Doctrine and Covenants section four. *"Remember faith, virtue, knowledge, temperance, patience, brotherly kindness, godliness, charity, humility, diligence . . ."*

"Actually, I might need a little work on the brotherly kindness," I said.

"I don't agree. You have honored your brother all the time I've known you."

"Except maybe for the kissing episodes."

"It takes two to kiss. He'll understand when we tell him."

"I hope so." I hesitated, wondering if I should say what I was thinking, but then decided to go ahead. "I didn't plan on falling in love with you."

"I know. Me, either."

"Awkward, huh?" I asked.

"Yeah."

"So what do we do?" I asked.

"We wait until Robbie comes home," she said softly.

"Yeah, that's what we do. Thank you again for not making a big deal out of me not getting you an actual birthday present."

She nodded. "Well, at first I did feel a little disappointed but then my dad talked to me. After I told him that I'd asked you not to get me a present, he goes, 'So how can you be mad at him for doing what you asked him to do?' I had to admit he did have a point."

"I owe him a big thanks."

She undid her seatbelt and slid over next to me. "Can I ask you a question?"

"Yeah, sure."

"Have you told your mom and dad about us?"

"Not much, except I've told them we see each other when I transport you, Sophie, and your harp to wedding receptions."

"So they don't know about us liking each other a lot?"

"No. I just thought it would be simpler that way. If I told them, they'd tell me I was not supporting Robbie on his mission, and they'd probably encourage me not to see you so much."

She nodded knowingly. "I can understand why you wouldn't tell them."

I didn't want to leave our little sanctuary in my pickup parked on some random gravel road. "Before we leave, can I tell you what I like about the way you look?"

"Why do you want to do that?" she asked.

"I might not ever get the chance again."

She opened her eyes wide. "I'm not sure if this is the right thing to do. I mean, in terms of us meeting at a family reunion when we're each married to someone else."

"Look, if it will relieve your mind, I'll move to Kenya with my wife and never come back."

"Well, that seems fair enough. Okay, go ahead."

"Is it okay, if in doing this, I touch your face to point out the area I'm describing?"

"You won't be touching my face with your lips, will you?"

"No, no! None of that! Right now I'm thinking either my right or left index finger. Certainly with me in the driver's seat, my right hand is nearer to you but it's actually at a bad angle in reference to you. Also, I'm always a little more comfortable using my left hand, except of course when I bat and then I can bat either left- or right-handed."

She snickered. "That's probably more information than I needed. I would say either index finger would be permissible."

"Okay, well here goes. The first place I'd like to take us is to your eyes. Do you know the color of your eyes changes a little based on what you're wearing? Sometimes they're like a shade of green, at other times they're more brown, and once in a while blue."

"You're not going to touch my actual eyes, are you? I only let an eye doctor do that."

"No. Next we come to your eyelashes. Whatever you do with them, it's working. It's a great combination. Eyes and eyelashes working together to make me a little light-headed. And then your eyebrows."

I turned and used my left index finger to trace each eyebrow. "These are like mood indicators to me. They tell me when you're mad or sad. When you're mad, you go into this scowl, and you get little furrows right here. Like a flag at half mast. But when you're happy, it's like a flag at full mast."

I touched her nose. "Now let's move on to your nose. I like your nose because it's a strong nose."

"Are you saying I have a big nose?"

"Yes, but in a good way. It's like the nose of a Greek princess."

"How much actual experience have you had with Greek princesses?"

"None. Don't distract me. Your nose shows strength of character. And let's not forget your lips. They are full and inviting, like grapes ready to be plucked."

She shook her head and smiled. "I can't tell if that's an insult or a compliment."

"A compliment," I insisted. "I wish I had experienced your lips more than I have."

"Want to go watch another soccer game?" she teased, but then quickly added, "Sorry, I didn't really mean that."

"If we were married, your lips would be like a safe harbor to come home to."

"Argh. Ahoy, there, matey! Welcome aboard!" she called out in her best pirate imitation.

"Exactly. And that leads us to your chin. Aye, it's a bold chin, Captain."

"I'll take your word."

"Let's go now to your hair. Good color, sheen, and usually well groomed."

She laughed. "Have you ever judged a dog show?"

"I love your hair. Now we proceed to your neck."

She scowled. "Whoa, there, Sports Guy! How far are you intending to go with this?"

"I'm stopping at the neck."

"Okay, proceed with extreme caution."

"I love to see your neck from the side when you're turning your head away from me. It's so amazing! All those clean lines! It's a great neck, really."

"Okay, we're done, right?"

"Yeah, we are, totally."

"Good."

We looked at each other for a long time.

"Let's drop everything else and just live here in your pickup," she said.

"I wish we could."

"Me too."

I sighed. "I'll miss you."

"I'll miss you, too. You're the best friend I've ever had."

"Same for me. Friendship is good," I said.

"Yes it is. Real good."

I didn't have much else to say. "I guess we'd better go."

"Yeah, maybe so."

She rested her head on my shoulder on our way home. We didn't explain it away because we both knew these times were coming to an end.

Robbie was coming home.

Chapter Six

Since January, I had been calling Nathan's dad every Monday afternoon to discuss with him what kind of special Hillman Auto Body Shop would be offering the next week. He usually didn't have anything in mind so I'd suggest something Nathan had done the previous year and that was fine with him.

All that time he'd never said much about his Web site. But near the end of April he did bring it up. "I just wanted you to know that the Web site is bringing in more business. Sometimes lately I've also had phone calls about your blog."

"Really? What do people say about it?"

"Mostly good things."

"Well, that's good. Do you ever go in and read what I've written?" I asked.

"No, not really." He paused. "I've had several women call and tell me thanks though. That it's helped them or their husband. They ask me to keep the blog going. One girl said

115

she really wanted to meet Steve-O. I told her I couldn't help her with that." He paused. "Are you Steve-O?"

"Sometimes."

"Well, I'll keep that to myself. Anyway, whatever you're doing, keep it up. Oh, another thing, Nathan says for me to tell you hello. He's doing real good. We're very proud of him."

"You should be."

This was my next blog.

> May 2
>
> I recently spent time at a wedding reception sitting next to a husband and his wife listening to them argue about some stupid thing. This is what I've learned from the experience:
>
> 1. You will never win an argument with the woman you love.
>
> Why? Because you're asking her to change how she feels about something. And for the most part none of us can change the way we feel. You can present one excellent point after another but most likely at the end of it, she'll still feel the same way. So, instead of arguing your case, try to find out how she feels.
>
> 2. Admit to yourself that you're not blameless. The excuses you make to her for your actions will most always carry some weakness.
>
> For example if you say you're working eighty hours a week for her, is that really true? If you weren't with her, wouldn't you still work eighty

hours a week? And if you only worked forty hours a week but spent more time at home, wouldn't you both be happier? Don't assume that the reasons you do things a certain way are necessarily valid.

3. Learn how to apologize.

Guys, listen to me. "I'm sorry you misunderstood what I said," is a bad apology. So is, "I'm sorry you got your feelings hurt."

Good apologies involve taking responsibility for what you did that was wrong. Here's an example. "I'm sorry I didn't call you and tell you I'd be late."

4. If you say you're going to change for the better, do it now. Give her a list of the things you're going to do and start immediately to implement them. Report back to her every day so she knows you're working hard to make the changes you said you'd make.

5. Never bring up past complaints or incidents.

If you ever say, "Yeah, what about what happened last year when you . . ." If either of you ever do so, it will evolve into a major fracture in your relationship. Focus on the current problem; never bring up past issues.

Although I wrote as if I knew what I was talking about, I began to have my doubts. Sometimes I felt like some kind of a relationship spy, sneaking around at wedding receptions, eavesdropping on the relationship blunders of people I didn't even know. How can you have any respect for someone like that?

Whatever made me think I had anything to say? I thought. *If I'm so smart in telling guys how to treat the women they love, then why am I about to lose the only girl I've ever loved? If I end up losing Brianna, what difference will any of this make?*

Sophie and Christopher got engaged a few days after April Conference. Their wedding date was set for Saturday, May 16 in the Provo Temple. Brianna began spending all her spare time helping Sophie with the details for the wedding reception.

The wedding ceremony was amazing, except I kept wishing Brianna had been with us in the temple. She had not received her own endowment yet so she had to wait outside for us to come out of the temple for pictures.

One good thing that happened in the sealing room just after the ceremony was that Sophie's mom spoke to me. She shook my hand, gave me a hug, and then said, "Thank you for being such a blessing to my daughter."

"I didn't do much."

"No, you did. You were an answer to my prayers. I will always be grateful to you. I will always think of you as Sophie's guardian angel, who Father in Heaven sent to help her to discover that there are men who are kind and gentle and faithful to their covenants. You are a big part of the reason she is getting married today. I really can't thank you enough."

I didn't know what to say besides "Thanks." More than anything, I was grateful that I'd been of some help to Sophie.

At the reception that night, Sophie and Brianna played a

couple of songs together. They were both in tears by the time they finished because they knew their friendship would now be changing.

After the reception I took Brianna back to her apartment. I think we were both reluctant to say what we were thinking, which was that it was getting so close to when Robbie would return home from his mission.

I told her what Sophie's mom had said to me inside the temple about me being like a guardian angel to Sophie.

"That's what you've been to me, too," she said, as I walked her up to her door. "Please hold me," she said.

I held her but not real tight. She was crying. I didn't ask why because I knew.

We couldn't say anything. We'd said it all.

As I drove back to my apartment, I had the feeling that the thing I'd treasured most in my life was about to come to an end.

After that, things changed between Brianna and me. What had once been only a vague concept became now a stark reality. My brother was coming home, and Brianna, the girl who had waited for him, might very well end up marrying him.

Because she might end up being my sister-in-law, our good-byes at night were now only high-fives or the kind of hug you'd give your sister. And now we both avoided even talking about Robbie.

I had now known Brianna longer than Robbie had known her when he left on his mission. I resented the fact that even though he didn't know her as well as I did, he was going to come back and take over. In my lowest moments, I regretted I'd even tried to be Brianna's friend.

Brianna and I now only took walks during the day. I think we were both worried about being alone with each other. My biggest concern was that, in a moment of weakness, I'd tell her how much I loved her, and ruin everything.

On our walks we mostly talked only about our classes, never about our feelings for each other. Once she thanked me for being such a good friend. I forced a smile and told her I was happy to be her friend. That was okay, but then I blew it when I said bitterly, "Anything for Robbie, right?"

"Yes, of course," she said much too quickly.

Brianna and I began to analyze everything we did together in terms of how we would explain it to Robbie. *What would Robbie think?* became our unexpressed standard for what we could do.

Brianna came up with a good activity that we could describe to Robbie without feeling defensive. Her mom had researched several hundred names of dead ancestors who were in need of baptism. Several times a week Brianna and I would go to the Provo Temple. I would baptize her ten or fifteen times and then afterward we'd stop on the way home and get something to eat.

We both felt safe in the temple. Because we were walk-ins, we usually joined a ward group of youth. We were glad to be around them. It kept us from holding hands or showing any affection to each other. Just what we needed in preparation for Robbie's return.

One week before Robbie came home, after I'd done all my homework for my classes, I didn't feel like doing anything so I decided to watch TV. I surfed cable channels and watched snatches of sitcoms. In one after the other, a guy and a girl on their first date ended up in bed together. After about twenty minutes of channel surfing, I turned it off and wrote this for my blog.

June 3

Guys, let's talk about how Christmas was when you were a boy. (Or at least how it was for me.) A few weeks before Christmas, your family decorated a Christmas tree. And then your mom put out a few decorations around the house to remind you that Christmas was coming. And maybe your family drove around town looking at the Christmas decorations. You might have had family coming for Christmas. There were special foods prepared. Your family probably had traditions you repeated year after year. Some families go caroling. Some visit nursing homes. Some give to families who have less than they do.

Christmas is a process. Much of the joy of Christmas comes from the preparations we make for it. Take away that preparation and anticipation, and you don't have much.

That anticipation heightens our enjoyment of the season. We don't rip open a Christmas present the second it is placed under the tree. We wait until Christmas. This delayed gratification enhances the actual event. Thirty days of preparation for one day of celebration.

This blog isn't really about Christmas. It's about the media's suggestions that what guys should

121

do is immediately become intimate with someone they hardly know and don't care that much
about.

So, guys, what reasons could there possibly be
for moving into the bedroom right after meeting
a woman? Because you can't dance? Because
you want to have something to brag about to
your buddies at work? Because you're not good
at carrying on a conversation? Because you
want to let a former girlfriend know you're totally over her?

Recreational sex is wrong on so many levels.
Even those who are not religious need to realize
that you're cheating yourself and your partner.
Not only that: a life lived that way will most likely
have very little joy because everything happens
too fast with no anticipation, no planning, and
no development of respect and admiration for
each other.

Guys, my advice is slow down and begin to appreciate the woman you're seeing. Appreciate
how she smiles, how she laughs, how she bowls,
how she crinkles her nose, even how she cares
about those around her. Don't rush things.
Court her, show kindness to her, listen to her,
fall in love with her, get engaged to her, marry
her, and then enjoy your time together.

Ask any kid who has sneaked an early look—
opening a Christmas present before Christmas
ruins the fun.

The day before Robbie got home, Brianna and I went once again to the temple to do baptisms.

While we waited for all the youth in our group to be baptized, we sat together on a bench outside the font.

"This is our last time doing baptisms before Robbie gets home," she whispered.

"I know."

"I want to say something to you here in the temple," she said quietly.

"Okay."

"Almost every day since we started spending time together, I've thanked Father in Heaven for sending you to help me."

That blew me away. All I could think to say was, "Thank you."

"You have been so kind to me, Austin. You've seen me at my worst. You've seen me sick in bed throwing up in front of you. And then you cleaned it up and washed my sheets and made my bed. I will never forget that. And that's not all. You've hauled me and my harp all over Utah and never complained. You gave me a priesthood blessing when I was sick. You've prayed with me. Also, because of Sophie, I feel like we've raised a daughter together."

"Yeah, me too, actually."

She reached for my hand. "You've shown me an example of what it means for a guy to honor his priesthood. I know that I could have called on you any time for a blessing and you'd have been worthy to do it. I am grateful for your good example."

"Thanks for saying that."

She choked up a little as she said, "I will always hold a place in my heart for you as my true and faithful friend."

"Yes, that's what we are, true and faithful friends," I agreed.

"Yes, and no matter what happens, promise we'll always be friends."

"I promise."

I baptized Brianna ten times and then, just before going up the stairs, we embraced. Both of us were in tears but that's one advantage of being completely drenched. Nobody can see your tears.

The ordinance worker in charge of the baptistry couldn't let it slide. He cleared his throat. "Normally we don't have people hugging each other in the font. It's a safety issue more than anything."

We looked at each other and smiled. "A safety issue, you say?" I asked.

"Yes. Like if one of you lost your balance and fell down and hit your head on the font."

"Thank you," I said. "We'll be careful." I sighed. "And, actually, the truth is, we'll never do this again." It gave me a sinking feeling in my stomach to say it.

That night, Brianna asked me for a blessing. I gave her one, although it was difficult for me to do because the more I assured her things would work out, the less hope I had for myself. So it was pretty much a generic blessing. I blessed her to have peace of mind, to have a happy marriage, and righteous children, and a life full of both happiness and challenge.

When I finished, she stood up and asked, "Can I have a hug?" We hugged for a moment. I would have continued, but

I think she felt guilty because she pulled away, thanked me, and said good night.

That was it. From now on we were on Robbie Standard Time.

The next afternoon Robbie was scheduled to fly into the SLC airport. I picked Brianna up at her apartment, and we drove to my folks' home.

Just after pulling into the driveway, before we got out of the car, I reminded her about Tornado the Monster Dog. "As soon as we step out of the truck, he'll start barking and come running at us, like he's going to attack us, but don't worry, his chain will stop him before he gets to us. And then I'll yell at him and tell him he's a stupid mongrel dog, and that will make him bark even more, and if we're lucky, his owner will open the door and yell for him to be quiet."

I opened my door, but Tornado just sat there.

I walked around and opened the door for Brianna. "Tornado isn't barking at us," she said.

"He must not have seen us. Let's walk around on the driver's side of the car."

We walked around. He stood up.

"He's still not barking," she said.

"This has never happened before. Maybe if I throw a rock or a stick at him, he'll try to attack us."

"Why would you even think about that? He seems like a nice dog to me."

With that Tornado wagged his tail. I swear, he almost looked as though he was grinning.

As I walked her toward the house, I turned back to him and muttered, "Stupid dog."

Brianna looked at me like, instead of Tornado, I was the one who was sick and twisted.

When we entered the house, my mom came running and threw her arms around Brianna. "Well, this is the day we've all been waiting for, isn't it?"

"Yes, of course." Brianna said weakly, glancing back at me to see how I was doing.

"You'll be staying in the same room as before," my mom told her. "Let me show you your towels."

I sat down on the couch and touched my head. I had such a headache and dreaded everything that was going to happen over the next few days. I felt like I was about to have a panic attack. Whenever that happened to me on my mission, if we had time, I'd take a long shower. That's what I needed now.

When they came back from our guest bedroom, my mom had Brianna sit down at our kitchen table. When I entered, she told me to sit down and eat.

"No, I'm not hungry. I think I'll take a shower."

"We don't have much time. Your dad is going to be here in a few minutes to take us out to the airport. Robbie's plane is scheduled to land in an hour and a half. We want to make sure we're there in plenty of time."

"I'll hurry."

I hurried downstairs and took a shower. It was great getting the room all steamed up and pretending that I'd never have to leave my shower.

Ten minutes later my mom called to me through the bathroom door, "Your dad's here! We need to go."

"Yeah, I'm almost ready."

I jumped out of the shower, dried as fast as I could, and threw on my clothes.

Five minutes later my mom yelled at me again through my bedroom door. "Austin, come on! We need to go!"

I grabbed a towel, put on my shoes. There was no time to put on socks, but I stuffed a pair into the pocket of my pants.

When I got in our minivan, the only place for me to sit was in the backseat next to Brianna.

I dried my hair on the way, but since I didn't have a comb, my hair ended up looking like I had an Afro.

"You don't have socks?" Brianna whispered to me.

"They're in my pocket."

I fished them out and began to put my socks on.

"Your hair makes you look like you're in disguise."

"You think so?" I asked hopefully.

I still had one secret I'd kept from her, and that was I'd been writing a relationship blog on the Web site for Hillman Auto Body Shop, and that some of what I'd written were based on things she and I had experienced. I thought she should find it out from me and not from somebody else. If I didn't tell her now, I might never do it.

"I have something I need to tell you." I reached for her hand.

"Please, Austin, not now. I'm nervous enough as it is."

"Okay, it can wait."

"Let go of my hand, okay?" she whispered. "Your mom might turn around and see us holding hands and that would be, well, I would think confusing to her."

"Yeah, sure. I forgot."

"One thing you should know. I'm not sitting next to you on the way back."

"No problem. I'll sit in back with the luggage," I said bitterly.

That made her mad. "Give me a break, okay? You don't have to sit in back with the luggage! Just don't sit next to me. I'll probably be sitting next to Robbie."

My chest hurt, and it was hard to breathe. I bent over and took a couple of deep breaths.

She touched my shoulder. "It's going to be okay," she said.

"Yeah, I know. We'll both get through this."

"Please let me work on your hair," she said. "You look like a terrorist." She used her fingers to try to get my hair in some kind of socially acceptable condition.

My dad found a place to park in Parking Lot A, and we took a shuttle bus to the terminal. Inside, we checked the flight on the arrival board and found it was on time. Then we went to the designated luggage carousel and waited.

I was standing next to Brianna. She leaned over. "I wish you could hold my hand," she whispered.

"Me, too, but like you said, that would probably freak out my mom and dad."

"Yeah, I know."

Robbie was one of the last passengers to come down the escalator. He was talking to a man wearing a business suit and carrying a laptop. At the bottom of the escalator, Robbie handed the man a pass-along card and shook his hand. Then he turned to look for us.

Picture Shaquille O'Neal in a missionary suit, and that's what Robbie looked like.

We hurried over to him. He kissed my mom, bear-hugged my dad, shook hands with Brianna, and then hugged me. Actually, he crushed the breath out of me.

He's going to kill me when I tell him about me kissing Brianna, I thought.

My mom took over after that, asking a million questions. Brianna and I tagged along after them.

"He doesn't even care that I'm here," she complained.

"Of course he does. But you have to remember he's still a missionary."

"When you came home, by this time we'd already hugged," she said.

"You hugged me, I didn't hug you."

"I didn't mean anything by it."

"I know that."

After claiming Robbie's luggage, we took the airport shuttle bus back to where the family car was parked.

"I call shotgun!" Robbie called out, just the way he'd always done, ever since he was ten years old.

Brianna looked over at me with a puzzled expression on her face.

So, now in the backseat, there was Brianna and me and my mom.

Robbie talked louder than he really needed to. He told us about the man he'd sat next to on the plane, the one we'd seen him give a pass-along card to.

I looked over at Brianna. She looked as though she was about to cry, so I held her hand.

"Thanks," Brianna whispered to me.

My mom noticed us holding hands. "Robbie's home now," my mom told me. "You don't have to be a . . . well

. . . such a good friend to Brianna anymore. She has Robbie now."

"Austin and I will always be friends," Brianna said to her.

My mom shook her head and sighed.

"Do you want me to tell you what my mission president said during my last interview?" Robbie asked.

Basically, in summary, his mission president had told him that he'd worked hard, that he'd blessed the elders he'd trained, that he'd been an exemplary zone leader, that he'd shown leadership in working with ward and stake leaders. That he'd *blah-blah, blah-blah, blah-blah.*

"Guess how many baptisms I had my last two months?" Robbie asked.

"Six," Brianna said softly.

Robbie didn't hear her. "I had six my last two months! In fact, I led the mission two months in a row."

"That's very good," I said to Brianna.

"Yes, I know," she whispered back. "He's told me all about it in his letters. In fact, that's all he tells me in his letters. Anytime somebody gives him a compliment, he's written me about it."

Brianna and I were both a little embarrassed by Robbie's bragging. "How's your brother Todd?" I asked Brianna over Robbie's victory-lap monologue.

"He's good. He talks about you a lot."

"Mainly about me giving you jerky for a birthday present, right?"

"Actually he focuses mainly on the Big Slurpy and, of course, the *Keep on Truckin'* hat."

"Guess who called me last night?" Robbie asked us and everybody in the cars around us.

"Who?" my mom asked.

"The football coach for Idaho State College. He wants me to play ball for him next fall. On a full-ride scholarship. Isn't that great?"

"That's so good!" Brianna said, but apparently Robbie didn't hear her.

"How did he hear about you?" my dad asked.

"Well, that is an interesting story. It seems that the coach has a daughter named Andrea serving in our mission, and after she saw me playing touch football with the other missionaries, she told her dad about me. He called my high school coach, got a good recommendation, and that was all it took."

I turned to Brianna. "Did you know anything about this?" I whispered.

"No, he didn't mention Andrea in his letters. How does he know her first name, anyway?"

"Beats me."

"Did you ever know the first names of any of the sister missionaries in your mission?"

"No. But I totally see how it could happen. Like if her last name was Jones, and there were like five Sister Joneses in the mission, then maybe even the mission president might start using their full names, so people would know who he was talking about."

"Did you have five Sister Joneses in your mission?"

"No. I just said that to maybe explain how he knows her first name."

"Ask him," she said softly.

"Ask him what?"

"What her last name is."

"Hey, Robbie, what's this sister missionary Andrea's last name?" I asked.

"Sepulski. Why?"

"No reason."

Brianna pursed her lips and leaned into me. "You think there were six Sister Sepulskis on his mission?"

"Probably not."

Brianna closed her eyes and reached for my hand again and squeezed very hard.

"My mom—" I started to say.

She turned to me. "I don't care. Please just let me hold your hand, okay?"

"Okay. Oh, there's another way he might know her first name. Maybe Andrea has already gone home, so then he might know her first name."

Brianna leaned forward. "Is Andrea still on her mission?" she asked Robbie.

"Yeah, she's got a little over a month to go."

I leaned into Brianna and whispered in her ear. "If you spend a lot of time with Robbie in the next month, I'm sure he'll totally forget all about her."

"Her dad wants me to stay with them when she talks in sacrament meeting," Robbie announced, speaking like he was calling signals at a football game. "And guess what else? Her dad told her there's a good chance I could be starting for them right away! Man, I'm pumped!"

"I have such a killer headache now. Please hold me," Brianna pled quietly.

"Actually, this might not be the best time, you know, for that."

My mom couldn't stand it anymore. She reached over and touched my shoulder. "I don't think you should be holding Brianna's hand now."

Oh, sure, blame me, I thought.

Brianna and I sat up straight and focused our attention on Robbie, who was continuing to inform us how magnificent he was.

When we pulled into our driveway and got out, Robbie spotted Tornado the Monster Dog, and ran over to him. "How's my boy?" He stuck his arm out and Tornado promptly opened his mouth and clamped down on it playfully.

"Who's your daddy? Am I your daddy? Yes, I am! Yes, I am! I'm your daddy! Yes, I am! I'm your daddy! And guess what? Daddy's home! Yes, I am! Good dog!"

Robbie ran next door and told the owner he was home from his mission and asked if he could untie Tornado and throw the ball for him to retrieve, like they had done before his mission.

The owner was so excited to see Robbie, he came outside with him. "Tornado's sure missed you!" he said.

"And I've missed Tornado! Every day I was gone! Yes, I did! I missed you! Yes, I did! I missed Tornado the Killer Dog! Yes, I did! Yes, I did!"

I looked at Brianna, who seemed to be taking this hard. "I'm sure he missed you, too," I said.

Robbie picked up a slimy, chewed-up tennis ball and threw it into the next yard. "Go get it, Tornado!"

Tornado raced for the ball and brought it back and laid it at Robbie's feet.

And then they did it again.

"This is not how I pictured things when Robbie came home," Brianna said softly.

My mom and dad went inside, but Brianna and I stood around and watched Robbie throw the ball for Tornado to retrieve.

"I could totally get that ball too, you know," Brianna whispered in my ear.

"Of course you could," I said.

The next time Tornado brought the ball back, Robbie held onto it. Tornado clamped down on it with his jaws. Robbie got down on his hands and knees and began yanking the ball back and forth, trying to see if he could pull it out of Tornado's mouth. Tornado growled, and, much to our surprise, Robbie growled back.

I'd had it. I went over to Robbie and said privately, "You need to pay attention to Brianna. I mean, after all, she waited for you for two years."

"Yeah, well, Tornado has been waiting for me, too. Haven't you, Boy? You've been waiting for me to get back, haven't you? Yes, you have! Yes, you have!"

Robbie hugged Tornado and then began to pet him. Tornado started licking Robbie's face.

Robbie was absolutely focused on that stupid dog. "That's my good dog! Yes, it is! That's my good dog!"

Brianna grimaced and shook her head. "That is so gross," she whispered to me. "His whole face is covered with dog spit."

"Yeah, it is, totally. But you know what? I bet it washes right off."

She brought her hand to her lips. "I'm not sure I'll ever be able to kiss him again."

This was good news for me. "You know what? I wouldn't blame you at all if you didn't. I read somewhere that some germs stay on a person's skin their entire life."

She looked into my eyes. "Please, Austin, make it stop."

I nodded and stepped over to Robbie. Tornado snapped at me but Robbie held him so he didn't bite my leg off.

"You and I need to take a walk!" I yelled at Robbie. "Without the stupid dog, okay?"

"He's not a stupid dog."

"Whatever."

Robbie hooked Tornado to his chain, and we began our walk.

"You need to pay attention to Brianna," I said.

"I haven't been released from my mission yet."

"You can still talk to her. Ask her questions about her family."

"Yeah, okay. One thing I was thinking about on the plane was she's never seen any of my trophies."

I groaned. "Are you serious? She doesn't care about that."

"That's easy for you to say. You don't have any trophies."

"Even if I did, I wouldn't show them to her. Especially not after I'd been away for two years serving a mission. Listen to me. She's a junior in college. You think she cares what anyone did in high school?"

"You think I should show her the letter from my mission president saying what a great missionary I was?" he asked.

"No, I don't, Robbie. I think you should show her that you care about people, that you're sensitive to the Spirit, that you worked hard on your mission, and that you appreciate her waiting for you. And, also, I think you should compliment her on the growth she's experienced while you've been gone."

None of this seemed to really get through to Robbie. He continued. "Let's see. I have three football trophies for being on the team, and two for baseball, and then one that I got my sophomore year for a Frisbee tournament." He paused. "Also, I could show her my baseball glove that I used when we won State."

I'd given up by then. "Yeah, sure, that'd be real good to show her all those things. Especially the trophy for the Frisbee tournament. That for sure will win her over."

"Wait a minute. I vaguely remember you writing and asking to borrow my baseball glove."

"Yeah, that's right."

"So, do you still have it? I'd like to show it to Brianna along with all my trophies."

"Why are we talking about some stupid baseball glove when we should be talking about Brianna?"

"What about her?"

"Do you have any idea how amazing she is? You're a lucky guy."

"Yeah, I suppose."

"I saw her a lot while you were gone, you know, just to make sure she was okay."

"Thanks."

I hesitated for a moment and said to him, "Oh, there is one little thing I should probably tell you. Uh, I did kiss her a couple of times while you were gone, but then we felt bad about it, so we stopped."

He stopped walking and turned to me. "Are you saying you made out with the girl who was waiting for me on my mission?"

"Okay, listen carefully. It was just one of those things that happen when you see a girl twenty or thirty hours a week for almost a year. I'm sure you can understand how a few kisses might occur in that length of time. This is something that just happened. I didn't plan it. And what's even better, for the past little while all we've done together is go to the temple and do baptisms. And temple work is so important, right? So, anyway, we're just friends now."

"Okay, I guess I'll let it go this time."

"Thank you. It won't happen again."

"Yeah, right. So, anyway, where's my baseball glove?"

"I'll get it back. I promise."

"Can you get it now?"

That made me so mad. "No, I can't get it now! What is wrong with you, anyway? Why does a stupid baseball glove take priority over Brianna?"

"Stupid baseball glove? Is that what you think it is? Listen to me. We took State my senior year. In the championship game, I had a double and two singles. I caught a line drive to end the game. And I did it with that baseball glove. Could we look for it as soon as I'm released?"

Suddenly I wanted to punish him. "You know what? I have no idea where your glove is. Actually the guy who borrowed it might have left it at the ballpark after a game, and that was over a year ago, but, you know what, we could still look for it."

"What? You lost my baseball glove!"

I couldn't believe it. He was madder about me losing his stupid baseball glove than he was that I'd kissed Brianna. Talk about misplaced priorities.

Sometimes I hate my conscience. I felt bad for lying to him. "Okay, look. What I just said about losing your glove isn't true. I pretty much know where it is. I'll get it for you real soon. Maybe even today."

"Okay, good."

"Can I ask you a question though? How can you be this shallow after serving a mission for two years?"

"You think I'm shallow?"

"Yes, I do."

"Well, let me ask you a couple of questions. How many baptisms did you have on your mission?"

"Not as many as you did."

"That's right. And I led the mission my last two months."

I gave up. "Yeah, you're right. I never did that. That's for sure. I was out of line. Sorry."

Not long after Robbie and I returned from our walk, he and my folks drove to the stake center so our stake president could release Robbie from being a missionary. Just before they left, I told my mom I'd ask Brianna to help me set the table for dinner.

As soon as they left, Brianna came out of her room. "I don't know him anymore."

"Yeah, well, it's been two years. Can you help me set the table?"

She nodded. "I can't believe he's planning on going to Idaho for Andrea's homecoming talk."

"He's probably not that interested in her. He's probably just going there because her dad wants him to play football for him in the fall."

"No, there's something else going on."

"No, I don't think so, but, even so, this must be a big disappointment to you." I thought it might be helpful to be philosophical. "Sometimes there are bumps in the road of life that we don't expect."

She glared at me. "Do you mind?" she snapped at me.

"Sorry."

"All the time he was writing me he never told me about this sister missionary," she said.

"He should have told you."

"That's right. He should have," she said.

"I think it was unconscious of Robbie not to tell you about Andrea."

She looked at me, snickered, and then burst out laughing.

"What?"

"It's not *unconscious*. It's *unconscionable*."

"That's what I meant."

She opened the refrigerator. "I'm starving."

"I can help you with that." My mom had prepared in advance what we would be eating. I pulled some of the bowls of food out of the refrigerator. "Okay, let me teach you something. The trick here is not to eat so much my mom knows we've had some, so we'll have to take a little and then smooth it over so she won't notice. So we take a little of this potato salad, and a piece of ham from the middle, and we eat it fast and then wash and dry the plate and the spoons."

"You've done this before?"

"Oh, yeah, all the time when she was Relief Society president and prepared meals for people who were sick. Every time I heard someone was sick, I cheered up knowing all the good food I'd get to sneak."

"You are bad!" she teased.

"Yes, that's me. Bad to the bone. And now you're a part of it. Welcome to the club!"

We giggled through our food and had everything back in place when we heard the garage door go up.

You can always tell when Robbie enters the house. He makes enough sound to be a small army. "Brianna, I need to talk to you!" he said.

We both hurried out to him in the living room as my mom and dad were coming through the door.

"I've been released now so I can properly hug you."

"Really?" she asked.

He came to her and threw his arms around her and squeezed. I noticed her wincing. And then he let her go and said, "My mom helped me see that I should forget all about Andrea, at least until I see how it goes with you. So let's talk."

They went into the backyard and sat at the picnic table. We could of course hear everything he was saying.

If Robbie had been applying for a job, what he was saying would have been appropriate.

He basically bragged about his achievements on his mission and then went back to all his honors in high school. Mostly sports awards.

The way he was talking to her was so wrong.

And then he told her that if it did turn out she was the one, he wanted to have ten kids. He also announced that he wanted them spaced two years apart, so they'd all have brothers and sisters to play with as they were growing up. That reminded me of when I'd written "Ten Things You Should Never Say to a Woman."

"He's doing it all wrong," I said to my mom as I carried the ham to the table.

"I know, but at least he's trying."

When they came in to eat, Brianna looked as though she were in shock.

After dinner, I asked to speak to Robbie privately.

I took him into my dad's office. "You're messing up big time. There's a blog I want you to read."

I opened the Web site and scrolled down to the blog about how not to talk to a woman. "Read this," I told him.

After he read it, he said, "Who writes junk like this, anyway?"

"That's not the issue. How much do you know about what she's been doing since you've been gone?"

"Well, one thing I know. You were making out with her while I was away."

"Oh, get over it, Robbie! At most it was only about eight kisses since I met her a year ago. That averages out to, what? About two-thirds of a kiss per month, right? And, if it's any consolation, we always ended up feeling guilty about it, too."

"Yeah, well, you should have felt guilty."

"Okay, let me tell you something. I do feel bad about it. Okay? So to make it up to you, let me help you impress

Brianna. I'll give you some advice. The first thing you've got to do is quit bragging about yourself and focus on her."

"Like what?" he asked.

"What do you know about her? What's her major? What classes did she take last semester? How many times has she gone to the temple for baptisms in the past month? What do you know about Sophie, her best friend from high school? How many times did she and Sophie play for wedding receptions since you've been gone? What kind of a guy did Sophie marry? Where were they married?"

"I don't know any of that but that's because I've been gone for two years. So what's your point?"

"You didn't ask her a single question when you were talking to her. You think that's going to make her believe that you value her, that you cherish her, that you are interested in her life? Remember this: it's not what you say, it's what you ask."

"Yeah, yeah."

"Don't blow this off, okay? Right now the most important thing you can do is pay attention to Brianna."

He yawned. "Anything else I did wrong?"

"I hardly know where to begin. How do you think it makes Brianna feel to hear you talking about some random sister missionary by the name of Andrea? Brianna has waited for you for two years. She deserves a little more gratitude from you for that."

"Yeah, okay, I got it."

The last thing I confronted him about was the talk he was going to give in sacrament meeting. "If you just brag about all your accomplishments, that will be the absolute worst thing you can do. You think anybody around here cares about you being a zone leader? Talk about the people you taught and baptized."

Brianna came in. "What are you guys doing in here?"

As a reflex action, I turned off the laptop. "Nothing!" I said quickly.

"Austin here was having me look at the Random Thoughts About Life blog," Robbie said with a scowl on his face.

She glared at me. "I thought you told me that was a porn site."

"No, are you kidding?" Robbie said. "It's advice to guys about girls they're seeing. It's got a lot of good stuff in it." He scoffed. "At least, according to Twinkle Toes here."

"Let me look at the blog," she said.

"No, no, it's just for guys," I said, standing up to leave my dad's office.

"The way you turned it off when I came in makes me suspicious that it really is a porn site," Brianna said.

"It's not a porn site," I said.

"Let me see it then," Brianna said.

Just then my mom invited us to have some dessert.

After dessert, Robbie took Tornado for a walk and then went into his room to get some sleep.

Brianna was kind of down so I suggested we play Monopoly.

It took until two in the morning for me to totally take all her properties and money.

"Okay, that's it. I win," I said.

"You rotten slumlord," she complained.

I slept until ten the next morning, I guess because I

hadn't been sleeping much lately due to worrying about what was going to happen when Robbie came home.

By the time I washed up and got dressed, it was almost eleven. My mom was gone, but she'd left me a note saying she'd gone shopping for Sunday brunch when all of Robbie's friends would be coming over after church. She also told me that Robbie had gone fishing with my dad.

I looked all over the house, but I couldn't actually find Brianna. Until I went into my dad's office to check my emails. She was there in front of my dad's laptop. As I got closer, I could see she was reading something from my blog.

I could tell she'd been crying because there was a box of tissues next to her and a bunch of used tissues on the floor.

"Hi," I said.

"Hi," she said in barely a whisper.

"What are you doing?"

She handed me a piece of paper with three columns down the page. The first column had the date the piece was written, the second column contained the subject covered, and in the third column she'd written how it related to what had happened to us during that time period.

"How do you explain this?" she asked.

She had me. "I wrote everything in the blog."

"You wrote about things that happened to us?"

"Well, yeah, I guess you could say that."

"You needed me to provide material for what you wrote, is that it? Tell me, did you think of me as your lab rat or as your gerbil? I know you're very much into gerbils."

I went to put my hand on her shoulder, but she pulled away and glared at me. "Don't touch me! And don't ever call me again! Do you understand?"

"Yeah, I understand."

Robbie came into the house. "Brianna, we're home!"

"We're in your dad's office!" Brianna called out.

Robbie found us. "Dad had to go back to work for about an hour. Austin, he'd like you to put some filler in the cracks in the driveway today. Okay?"

"I guess."

"Brianna, look at this." He shoved a dead fish to about six inches from Brianna's face. "Isn't this a beauty?"

"Yeah, it's . . . it's . . . real good."

"Oh, one other thing, if you're not doing anything, you want to see my trophies from high school?"

I groaned.

"Uh, I guess so," Brianna said.

"Actually, they're in my room. My dad made me a trophy case while I was on my mission."

"I wouldn't feel good about going in your bedroom with your folks gone."

"Really? Why's that? You had no problem making out with Austin here while I was on my mission, did you?"

Brianna stood up, walked toward him, and got in his face. "Two years is a long time, okay? Listen to me! If your trophies and the fish you caught and me making out with Austin is all you've got to talk to me about, then I'm going back to Provo!"

Robbie, being such a competitive guy, could see he was losing the game. He began pacing the floor, his head down, trying to come up with a better game plan. After a short time, he stopped, smiled, and looked over at Brianna. "What were your favorite classes that you took while I was gone?"

Brianna seemed surprised. She sat down again and started to tell him about her classes.

At first I thought that Robbie had taken to heart all I'd tried to teach him, but then I noticed him glance at a fly fishing magazine. He would look at her like he was totally interested and then drop his gaze to read the teasers on the cover.

But Brianna didn't seem to notice so I figured she was buying it.

That was totally depressing. I wanted to warn Brianna that he was only following advice I'd given him, but I didn't because maybe what he was doing would make Brianna happy. I didn't want to ruin any chance of happiness for Brianna, even if it was with my clueless brother.

Actually there was another reason. I actually did feel guilty for betraying my brother's trust.

I got up, went into the bathroom, took a couple of aspirin, and trudged to my room and lay down on my bed and stared at the ceiling.

After a while, my mom came into my room and told me they were eating, but I told her I wasn't feeling very well and probably would just take a nap.

The next morning I drove to Provo and went to my apartment, did some homework, and wrote what I thought would probably be my last blog.

June 12

What does it mean when we say a guy is using a woman?

I'm not a guy who does things like that, so it has been hard for me to admit the possibility that I might be guilty of using a woman for material for the blogs I've been writing on this Web site.

I never thought of it that way. I mean, I really do care for this woman. I think we would both say that we were good friends. It's just that sometimes I would pick up some little insight from being with her, and I'd use that insight as the basis for this blog.

I've learned so much from her. Like when she told me not to get her anything for her birthday, so I didn't. When she had the flu and hurled in her bed, I cleaned it up and washed and dried her sheets and blankets for her. Maybe she realized then that I was her true and faithful friend.

In time she learned that I would do anything for her, including hauling her harp from one wedding reception to another in my pickup truck, then wrestling it out of the truck and into the hall. And then repeating the whole process again to get her back to her apartment.

She has accused me of spending time with her just so I'd have something to write about on my blog. I guess in a way that's true. The thing is, I've learned so much from her I just wanted other guys to know about it.

But now that she's found out about my blog, she's told me never to call or contact her again.

My question for you is, What do I do now?

From Alexis:

> Steve-O, Sugar Boy, forget all about her and come to Momma!

From Mattie:

> Just because a girl says "don't ever call me" doesn't mean you shouldn't call her. Call her right now, Steve-O! And keep calling her so she'll know how much you care about her. And if she still won't talk to you, go visit her. Don't give up.

From Jake:

> Move on, Dude! She's not worth it! If she says don't call, then don't call. Don't let her see you whining for another chance! Have some respect for yourself!

From Naomi:

> Hey, Steve-O, you moron, this blog isn't that great. Give it up and pour all your attention into this sweet woman. Nobody really cares if you ever write another word or not. Grow up, okay?

I stayed in my apartment Saturday night. On Sunday I drove home just in time to attend our ward's sacrament meeting so I could hear Robbie's talk.

He did everything right. He told about the people he'd taught and baptized, he used scriptures to help us understand the principles behind the stories, and he bore his testimony.

I was proud of him, and, of course, so was Brianna, although I wasn't sitting next to her.

After the three-hour block, we had visitors come for lunch. Rather than hang around and be in the way, I excused myself early and drove back to Provo.

I didn't call Brianna that entire week, nor did she try to get hold of me.

I did call my mom, though. She told me that Robbie and Brianna were seeing each other almost every day. After Robbie finished work, he'd drive to Provo Canyon, go fishing, and then afterwards, drop by and see Brianna.

I felt like what they say at the end of old western movies: *My work here is done.*

Chapter Seven

Two weeks after I'd last seen Brianna, on a Saturday morning, there was a knock on the apartment door. I was still asleep, but one of my roommates answered it and then came to my room to wake me up. "Brianna's here," he told me.

"Oh, great," I complained. "What does she want now?" I looked at the clock. It was seven-thirty in the morning on the only day I could sleep as long as I wanted.

"I guess you'll have to ask her that."

"I know what she wants," I grumbled. "She probably got herself another flute player, and she has a wedding reception to play for, and she needs me to haul her harp. Why me, you know what I'm saying? Why not get my brother Robbie to do it? No, that's not possible. Robbie and my dad are probably off fishing all day. 'So leave it to Austin, right? He does all the grunt work in our family.' Just like it's been my whole life. Let me tell you something. If you have a brother who loves to fish as much as your dad does, you're going to spend most of your life doing their work while they're gone fishing."

He really didn't care about any of that. "You want me to have her come in and wait?" he asked.

"Yeah, I guess."

I threw on some clothes and made my way to our five-foot by five-foot living room.

Brianna looked so beautiful it nearly made me sick to my stomach.

"What time do you need me tonight to haul your harp?" I asked grumpily.

"It's good to see you, too," she said as a form of reproof. "I didn't come here to ask you to haul my harp."

"Then why *did* you come here?"

"Last night Robbie and I had a talk . . . and . . . well . . . it's not going to happen."

"Why not? He's got lots of trophies."

"He's shown me everything except for the baseball glove. He says you still have that."

"Yeah, I need to get that back to him." I paused. "So why did you come here if you don't need a ride to a wedding reception?"

"To tell you about Robbie and me." She looked uncomfortable. "I thought you'd want to know. But maybe I was wrong."

She was still standing in the doorway to my apartment, looking very nervous, as though she were sorry she had come. I should have felt sorry for her, but my first reaction was anger. How dare she come here, expecting me to take her back and forget that for as long as I had known her, I'd always been her second choice? I wanted to punish her, to tell her she'd missed her chance. I wanted to tell her she was too late and that I'd moved on.

But I realized that might not be the wisest thing to do. I needed time to think.

"Do you want to sit down?" I asked.

She hesitated then said, "No, thank you. I should be going."

"I was just about to take a shower. Can you give me a few minutes?"

"Okay. How about if I go back to my apartment and you drop by when you're ready. Maybe we could take a walk or something?"

"Yeah, maybe so. I'll just be a few minutes."

As soon as she left, I called Robbie.

"Yeah?" he answered.

"Where are you?"

"I'm fishing with Dad."

"It figures. Did you and Brianna break up last night?"

"Yeah, how'd you know?"

"She told me this morning. What would you think if I started seeing her again?"

"I think that would be a big mistake."

"Why?"

"Because you've never been very good at taking care of my things."

"What are you talking about?" I asked.

"You lost my baseball glove, so who knows what you'd do with her?"

"Oh, yeah? Well, what about your gerbil? If it weren't for me, you'd have killed it."

"Brianna is not a gerbil, okay?" he said. "Hold on! I've

got a bite!" He set the phone down while he was reeling in a fish. When he came back on the line, he said, "Man! That was a lunker. You should see it."

I ignored his bragging. "What did you do to make her want to break up with you?" I asked.

"Me? It wasn't my fault. Nothin' I did ever made her happy. I bought her a fly rod. I taught her how to cast. And for what? She didn't even want to go fishing with me."

"You haven't been reading my blog, have you?"

"Are you crazy? Why would I do that?" he asked.

"Listen, I want to start seeing Brianna again. What do you think about that?"

"I'll tell you what. You find my baseball glove first and then we'll talk about Brianna."

"Fine then, I'll find your stupid glove. If I do, will you be okay if I start seeing Brianna again?"

"We'll see. Whoa! I got another fish on my line! Hold on."

I could hear my dad telling Robbie what a great fish it was.

A minute later, he was back to me. "I got me a nice three-pound rainbow trout."

"I'm happy for both of you."

"Ah, this is the life, out here in the sunshine, out on a boat, fishing. It beats writing lame advice to guys about how to treat a girl. You know what? I'm too embarrassed to tell any of my friends about what you've been doing."

I decided to ignore that comment. "Okay, picture this. It's ten years from now. We're at a family reunion. Me with Brianna and our kids and you with Mrs. Fish Lady along with your ten bratty kids. Are you going to feel resentful, seeing Brianna there with me?"

"Oh, man, I got another one! Hold on again, okay?"

He took so long I decided to shave while I waited for him.

"Okay, I'm back. I wish you were here so you could have seen me haul this one in."

"What a thrill that would have been," I said dully.

"Okay, I forgot what we were talking about. You asked me a question. What was it again?"

"I think you just answered it. Talk to you later."

I finished shaving and took a twenty-minute shower. While getting dressed, I reread my blog about how to treat a woman. That calmed me down enough so I ended up not wanting to punish Brianna for leaving me to see how things might work between her and Robbie. Especially when that's what I had encouraged her to do.

When I picked Brianna up, I told her I wanted to take her back to my folks' home. From the big smile on her face, I think she got the wrong idea—like I was going to propose to her or something. But at that time it didn't occur to me that's what she thought might happen.

We pulled into the driveway, and she hopped out of the truck and started up the walk toward the front door.

"Where are you going? We need to clean the garage," I said.

She looked disappointed. "We do?"

"Yeah. That's why I brought you here."

"Oh," she said softly. She seemed kind of down after that.

"Okay, first thing I need to do is pull out all my boxes

and go through each one," I said. "While I'm doing that, why don't you sweep the floor? You might want to hose it down first so it's not so dusty while you're working."

She looked confused.

"You're not afraid of a little work, are you?" I asked.

"No, I guess not."

"Good. Let's get started then."

After she finished sweeping the garage floor, I had her hang the tools back up on the hangers where they belonged. And then, after she finished that, I had her apply some cement-like filler to the cracks in the driveway.

Brianna was on her hands and knees filling in the cracks. At one point, she noticed I was sitting on the lawn reading my high school yearbook and complained, "Hey, this is not a library, okay?"

"Oh, yeah, I was just reading what a girl in my chemistry class wrote. Listen to this: 'I'll never forget how much fun it was sitting next to you. You actually made chemistry fun! Thanks for everything!'"

Brianna wasn't impressed. "So what? I wrote the same thing to like twenty guys in my senior class. Don't take it too seriously."

"No, I think she had a big crush on me."

"Did you make her fill in the cracks in your driveway, too?" she asked sarcastically.

"No, but if I had, she would have had a better attitude than you do."

"Why are we here?" she asked.

"I'm looking for Robbie's baseball glove."

"It's on the shelf over there," she said. "Behind the picnic basket."

"No, it isn't. Don't you think I would have looked on the shelves first?" I asked.

She got up, walked into the garage, went to the shelf, moved the picnic basket, grabbed Robbie's baseball glove, and tossed it at me.

"This is it! We found it! Good job!" I said.

"So, are we done?"

"Actually, if you could finish the section you're working on, then I'm sure my dad would be happy. He's been on me to do this for months."

She picked up the gallon container of filler, carried it over to me, and shoved it into my midsection. "There you go. Be my guest. I'll be inside talking to your mom."

So I had to finish up the job for her.

When I walked into the kitchen, my mom and Brianna were laughing.

"What's so funny?" I asked.

"Nothing," they both said at the same time with big grins on their faces. Which meant they had been talking about me.

My mom and Brianna worked on fixing lunch while I went out into the garage and bagged up all the things from high school I no longer wanted and put them into the garbage. Then I returned the few boxes left to the shelves where I'd gotten them.

When the three of us were having lunch, I remember thinking how natural it seemed for Brianna and me and my mom to be together.

After lunch my mom told us she had to go shopping. "Will you two be okay here all alone in the house?" she asked.

Brianna smiled. "We're always okay when we're together. It doesn't matter if we're alone or in a crowd."

Mom gave Brianna a knowing glance and a smile. "Of course. That's what I would have predicted."

And so my mom left to do her shopping.

"What do you want to do now?" I asked.

"I don't know. How about if you tell me about high school?"

"Why do you want to know?"

She smiled at me. "It's something I learned from a blog I recently read."

"Not much to tell. Robbie was like a sports legend his senior year, but I was gone on my mission by then."

"I want to know about your senior year."

"Okay. I'll go get my high school yearbook."

We were about halfway through it when Robbie and my dad came home.

"What's she doing here?" Robbie asked when he walked into our living room.

I stood up and handed him his baseball glove. "There it is, are we even now?"

He looked carefully at the glove and then glared at me. "You used this for softball, didn't you?"

"Not personally. I loaned it to a friend who used it for softball."

"Look at this! The pocket is now bigger than it used to be. If I use this now for baseball, the baseball will just fall out."

"You're not playing baseball now."

"I could though. I could even play semi-pro ball."

"If you play semi-pro ball, I'm sure they'll give you enough money to buy a new glove."

Robbie was still inspecting the glove. "The guy you loaned this to never applied oil to the glove, either, did he? Gloves need oiling to keep the leather soft and pliable."

"You never told me to oil the glove."

"Well, I would think that would go without saying. Everybody knows you need to oil the glove."

"I didn't know that. Look, you got your glove. Are we even now?"

He frowned and then nodded. "Okay, I got the glove, so you can have Brianna."

Brianna was stunned. "I need to go now," she said in a little girl voice.

She walked out to my pickup and got in and waited for me to take her back to Provo.

"Now look at what you've done!" I complained to Robbie.

"What are you talking about? That was our agreement, wasn't it?"

"Robbie, sometimes you're a complete idiot."

At first, on the way back to Provo, Brianna wouldn't even talk to me. When I asked her a question, she would just shake her head and turn away from me.

I tried to explain. "Okay, look, this was all Robbie's idea, okay? I would never have come up with such a stupid idea that if I found his baseball mitt he'd be okay with me seeing you again. To me you're much more important than, well . . . a baseball glove."

She shook her head and turned those wonderful eyebrows of hers into a frown.

"The truth is, you're the best friend I've ever . . ." I began.

She reached over and turned on the radio so loud it would be impossible for me to talk to her.

That made me mad. I decided to leave it on even though it was so loud it was almost painful.

Actually, it was a baseball game. I was starting to get into it when she reached over and turned it off.

"Like I was saying . . ." I began.

"Don't talk to me!"

I didn't say anything else until I was taking one of the exits for Provo. If I didn't say something soon, I'd miss my chance.

"Look, there are some things I need to tell you. You don't have to do anything but listen to me, okay?"

She gave me no indication she'd even heard me.

"Okay, the thing is, you're my only friend. Well, that's not exactly true. I mean, I do have other friends. My room-mates maybe are friends, I guess, except I don't like to talk to them very much and we'll never talk to each other after we're no longer roommates. And, well, there's Sophie. She's a friend. But the thing is she's only a friend because of you. Also, there's the girl who wrote in my yearbook about how much fun she had sitting next to me in chemistry. I'm sure we were friends, but not so much now I guess. We haven't talked since we graduated from high school. But look, it's not like I'm some pathetic loner guy who doesn't have any friends. They just come and go, that's all."

"Are you done yet?"

I could tell from her expression that she just wanted to get away from me. But that only made me try harder and talk faster. "I guess in a way, life is like a conveyor belt where friends come into your life and then after a while they drop off into a box. You know, like a conveyor belt in a factory."

She groaned and then shook her head again.

I had now reached the stage of ranting. "Okay, it's not exactly like a conveyor belt! It's more like an auto assembly line, I guess, where they put parts on the car as it goes by. You know, the parts are like the things we learn from our friends that stay with us . . . until we roll off the assembly line . . . of life."

"The assembly line of life?" she asked, totally mocking me.

I had purposely missed the turn to her apartment just to buy me some time.

"Take a left at the next corner," she said.

"Okay, this is what I really want to say. You're the kind of friend that when I wake up in the morning, I can hardly wait to see you again. And when I leave you at your door at night, I wish I could be your roommate."

"Yes, I bet you do," she grumbled.

I finally figured where I'd gone wrong. "Not in that way," I added.

"Not in what way?" she snapped

"Not the way you were thinking of."

"How do you know what I was thinking?" she snapped.

"Well, actually, I don't."

"You think I go around thinking about that in regard to you?" she asked.

"No, of course not. We're just friends. And friends don't let friends, you know, uh, sleep together. Which I've never thought about in reference to you."

"If you've never thought about it, then how come you just said it?" she asked.

"What?"

"To say something you first must think about it," she said.

"I'm perfectly aware of that."

I pulled into her driveway. "Okay, can we talk?" I asked.

"No! This has been enough talk for me. In just a couple of hours you've forced me into doing manual labor involving cement, which is now drying on my fingers. I'll be trying to get it off for the next week. And then I find out you and your brother traded me for a baseball glove. And to top it off, you just told me you've thought about sleeping with me. You're really at the top of your game today, aren't you?"

As she hurried up the sidewalk to her door, I jumped out and yelled at the top of my voice, "I never actually said I wanted to sleep with you!" That alone would have been bad enough, but, out of spite, I foolishly added, "So don't get your hopes up, okay?"

There were like maybe ten girls who lived in her apartment building who heard me say that. They all turned to stare at us. It was then I knew what the gossip in her ward was going to be for the next week.

Brianna slammed the apartment door so hard the wind chime hanging next to it fell to the ground with a multi-toned crash.

So, all in all, it wasn't one of my best days.

Chapter Eight

On Sunday I texted Brianna like ten times and apologized for "everything I've ever done to make you mad."

On Monday, after rereading my advice in my blog, I texted her again, this time listing the things I'd done wrong and apologizing for each one. I also sent her a dozen roses.

On Tuesday I sent her a box of chocolates.

Tuesday afternoon I sent her a four-page letter, detailing what I'd done wrong.

On Wednesday morning I texted her again and assured her the last thing I would ever want would be to sleep with her.

On Wednesday afternoon I revised my earlier text message by adding that if we were married, then, of course, I would want to sleep with her. You know, just in case she was wondering if I was indeed normal in that area of life.

On Thursday morning, I texted her again that all I had meant to say to her was that at night, when I would leave her, I would sometimes wish I could be her roommate, which is of course not the same as saying that I wanted to sleep with her. At least it isn't in the same context as when a guy usually says that to a woman.

On Friday morning she called me and asked if I'd be willing to go to the temple and baptize her for some more of her family names.

I hadn't expected that, but I said I would be very happy to do that for her.

It was awkward being with her until we were sitting next to each other outside the baptismal font, waiting our turn and surrounded by a youth group.

"Thank you for all your many apologies during the week," she said quietly.

"I meant every word."

"I know."

"Are we still friends?" I asked.

"I don't know. Maybe."

"Good. That's very important to me."

"Me too, actually."

"I hope that no matter what happens we'll always stay in touch," I said.

"Do you mean that?" she asked.

"Yes."

"Always?" she asked.

"Yes, always."

"Even like ten years from now?" she asked.

"Yes, even ten years from now or even twenty or thirty."

She sighed. "There's only one way for that to happen," she said.

"What's that?"

"Well, we can't be best friends if we're each married to someone else, can we?"

"Oh, I see your point. No, we can't," I said.

"You're not perfect, Austin. Far from it, in fact."

"I know."

"But even so, you're the best friend I've ever had," she said.

The officiator turned to us. "You two want to be next?"

"Can you give us a few more minutes?" I asked.

She continued. "I've thought a lot about us this week. And I've prayed about it, too. So what I've come up with is a suggestion for you."

"Okay," I said.

"This is my suggestion. You might want to consider asking me to marry you."

I was stunned. That had never happened to me before, especially at the baptistry. "I'm not sure I heard you right."

"I said, that if you really and truly want us to be best friends forever, we'll have to be married. I see no other option."

My heart was racing. "Yeah, I suppose that's probably right. It's not that I haven't ever thought about it before," I said.

"That's probably a good thing."

I leaned toward her. "Would you say yes if I asked you to marry me?"

She gave me a teasing grin. "There's only one way to find out."

"Okay. Will you marry me?"

"Do you love me?" she asked.

"Oh, my gosh, are you serious? I love you more than

I can even say. Like if you were a ton of chocolate and I were a, well, a big blob of vanilla ice cream, for example. Then—"

She put her fingers on my lips. "Please stop, okay? So far your analogies have only gotten you into trouble."

"You're right. Let me just tell you that I love you very much."

She let out a sigh of relief. "That's good. I was afraid that this was only a good friendship."

"That's what love is, isn't it? An amazingly good friendship." I paused. "Do you love me?"

"Oh, yes, with all my heart."

"Then we really should get married."

"You're right." She nodded. "I accept your proposal."

"Does that mean yes?"

"It does."

I stood up and announced to everyone in the baptistry. "Brianna and I are going to get married! Isn't that great?"

The girls in the ward youth group broke into big smiles and looked thrilled. The boys not so much.

An elderly temple worker misunderstood why I was announcing that in the baptistry. "Actually, uh, you'll need to go upstairs for that."

We let a few more youth go ahead of us and then the officiator told us, "Okay, I've been patient with you two, but it's your time now."

We both stood up, holding hands. I gazed into Brianna's beautiful eyes. "Yes, it is. It's our time," I said.

"And our eternity," she added.

And you know what? So far it has been.

About the Author

Jack Weyland has long-since secured his place as the foremost LDS young adult novelist. The author of some 27 best-selling books, he has entertained and inspired generations of readers. After his retirement as a professor of physics at BYU-Idaho, he and his wife, Sherry, served a full-time mission on Long Island. The Weylands have five children and twelve grandchildren and reside in Rexburg, Idaho.